As ever, for Suzanne & the Two Terrors ...

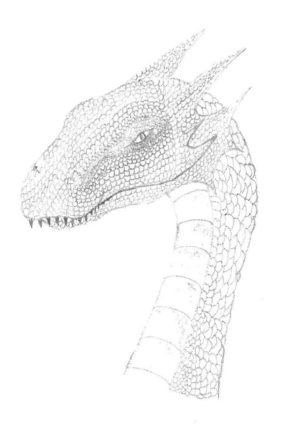

MEDIEVAL MADNESS

P.J. JOVANOVIC

CHAPTER
ONE
(the boy who was bored)

Thomas Tinkler was bored. He'd played on his XBOX for an hour – the maximum amount of time his parents allowed him in a day – and now he was wondering what else he could do to entertain himself. Slouching on the settee in the living room, he folded his arms across his chest and stared blankly ahead.

'Why don't you play with one of your board games?' his mother suggested, hovering at his side. 'Your brother's in his bedroom. Go up and give him a game of Monopoly; I'm sure he'd love that.'

'Finlay is seven years old,' Thomas said, pushing tumbles of thick brown hair away from his fringe. 'He won't be able to play properly.'

'Of course he will, if you show him.'

'I *don't* want to show him.'

'Okay, fine, Mr Grumpy. What about reading a book?' Mrs Tinkler went to the bookcase in the corner of the room and began perusing the shelves. 'Have you read the Chronicles of Narnia? That's pretty good. It's different tales about kids travelling to magical worlds.'

'I don't want to read a book.'

'What about the Harry Potter series? Even I enjoyed that. It's got wizards and unicorns and dragons and all sorts of weird and wonderful things. What more could you ask for?'

'I *don't* want to read a book,' Thomas said. He pooched out his bottom lip and stamped his foot sullenly. 'They're boring.'

'Boring?' another voice said. Thomas's dad entered the room. With a newspaper in one hand and a cup of tea in the other, he regarded his son with an inquisitive look. 'What's boring?'

'Books, apparently,' Mrs Tinkler said, rolling her eyes.

'Oh,' Mr Tinkler said. 'You obviously haven't been reading the right ones, son.'

'Just lately, he hasn't been reading *any*,' Mrs Tinkler put in.

'Oh,' Mr Tinkler said again. 'Well that needs to change.'

'It's going to,' Mrs Tinkler said, levelling a finger at Thomas. 'Starting this evening. You're sitting down with me at the table and reading a chapter of a book, any one of your choice – and you're not getting up until you've finished. Have you got that, young man?'

As grumpy and moody as he felt, Thomas knew better than to defy his mother when she was levelling a finger at him. He muttered a sullen, 'Yes.' His arms were still folded, his bottom lip still pooching out.

'I'm sorry,' Mrs Tinkler said. 'I didn't quite hear that.'

'*Yes!*' Thomas said, more loudly.

'Good,' Mrs Tinkler said. 'Now unfold your arms, sit up straight and don't look so miserable. You're a big boy now – ten years old – so start acting like it.'

He unfolded his arms, sat up straight, but just couldn't bring himself to not look miserable.

'Why don't you go out with your friends?' Mr Tinkler said. 'Go to the park on your bike.'

Mrs Tinkler gestured towards the window. 'It's raining,' she said. 'Have you even looked outside this morning?'

'You know what I'm like on a Sunday,' Mr Tinkler replied. 'My brain doesn't even start working before eleven a.m.' He mulled things over for a second, then said, 'How about a trip to the play centre? It'll get us all out of the house. Me and your mother can sit down and have a chat, whilst you and your brother work off some energy. Whaddaya say, kiddo?'

Thomas wasn't impressed at all. He could think of better things to do: like playing on his XBOX, for instance.

'Don't tell me,' Mrs Tinkler said to him, 'you think it's boring, yes?'

'A bit,' he said, glancing wistfully towards his games console.

'Err, don't even think about it,' Mrs Tinkler said. 'Your dad has come up with a good suggestion and that's what we're going to do.'

'Fine,' Thomas mumbled. 'Whatever.'

'Can you go and tell your brother what we're doing, please,' Mr Tinkler said to him. 'I'm sure he'll be happy about it.'

And he was, too. Bounding down the stairs, with Thomas following behind him, Finlay swept into the living room like a mini tornado.

'We're going to the play centre!' he said, jumping up and down with a huge grin on his face. 'Yippee! We're going to Tumble Kids!'

'Not if you don't get your shoes on and brush your hair, you're not,' Mrs Tinkler said to both her sons.

####

Fifteen minutes later, they were on the road, chugging along in Mrs Tinkler's battered old VW Beetle.

'How long are we staying there?' Thomas enquired from the back seat.

Finlay, who was seated next to him, said, 'Two hours, please!'

'Noooo!' Thomas said, glaring sideways at his brother. 'Just an hour – that's enough.'

'We'll pay for an hour and see how we go,' Mrs Tinkler said, dropping the Beetle down to second gear and pulling into the car park. 'We can always pay for another hour, if needs be.'

Both boys seemed happy enough with that.

As they all got out of the car, Finlay looked towards the play centre and let out a gasp of surprise. 'Whoa!' he said. 'How cool is that!'

Thomas followed his gaze and saw that the TUMBLE KIDS sign that'd been above the entrance had been replaced with another:

But this wasn't what Finlay was gasping at. It was the mural that'd been painted on the front of the building that'd got him excited:

'Check out that knight,' Mrs Tinkler said. 'And that castle, too.'

'The place must be under new ownership,' Mr Tinkler said. 'I bet it's all been refurbished.'

'Only one way to find out,' Mrs Tinkler said.

Thomas was now eager to get inside and take a look around. He didn't want to show that he was eager, though. He had gone to so much trouble today to emphasize how bored he was and didn't want to admit that coming to the play centre was now looking like a good idea.

Once they were all inside, Thomas was surprised to note that the place was almost empty. Only two of the tables in the seating area were occupied and no more than half a dozen children were in the play area, as far as he could see.

While they waited to be served at the check-in desk, Mrs Tinkler said, 'I love how the play area has been designed so it looks like a castle. Check out those turrets. There's even slit holes to shoot arrows through.'

Finlay bounced up and down with excitement. He stood on his tiptoes so he could look over the entry gate. 'What are we waiting for?' he said. 'I want to go in! Want to go in!'

'Hullo!' Mr Tinkler said, leaning across the check-in desk, trying to get someone's attention. 'Service, please! *Service!*'

From a room at the back, a man with a shock of curly grey hair stuck his head through the doorway and looked around. He noted where the voice had come from and sauntered over to greet his new customers.

'Well hello there,' he said, smiling warmly. 'Sorry to keep you waiting; I was just preparing some food in the kitchen.'

'Hello,' Mr Tinkler said, greeting the man back. 'When did this place open? We came here a couple of months ago, when it was Tumble Kids. Any idea why they ceased trading? It's always been busy when we've been here, so I can't imagine it was because of a lack of custom.'

'The previous owner had to quit due to unforeseen personal circumstances,' the man explained. 'I stepped in and bought the business from him, then did it out to my own tastes. What d'you think? D'you like the medieval theme?'

'*Yesssss!*' Finlay said. 'It's wicked!'

'And what about you, young sir?' the man said, focusing his attention on Thomas. 'D'you like it?'

Managing a shrug, he replied, 'It's okay.'

The man looked a little taken aback. 'Just okay?' he said. 'That's not quite the reaction I was hoping for, I must admit.'

'Don't take any notice of my grumpy son,' Mrs Tinkler said. 'He's on a mission today to be as miserable as possible, I'm sure.'

Thomas said, 'I am not!'

'Yes you are,' Finlay put in.

'I am *not!*' Thomas repeated, more forcefully.

'Oh yes you are,' Finlay said with a mischievous glint in his eyes.

'Enough!' Mrs Tinkler said, raising a cautionary finger. 'I don't want to hear another word from the pair of you. And neither does this nice man. We've only just brought you pair in here and already you're causing a ruckus.'

'It's okay,' the man said. 'It's not a problem, really.' He focused his attention on Thomas. 'I *guarantee* that you'll have an exciting time here. By the time you leave, your heart will be pumping hard and

adrenaline will be pulsing through your veins, my
little friend. Oh yes yes *yes*.'

'What's adrenaline?' Thomas said, perplexed. He
wasn't keen on the way the man was looking at him.
It was like he knew something that Thomas didn't.

'It's a substance that's released into your blood
when you're feeling strong emotions,' Mr Tinkler
said. 'It makes your heart beat faster, so you have
more energy.' Looking around, taking in the place, he
changed the subject. 'This place should be a lot busier
than this on a wet Sunday. It should be heaving.'

'We only opened a few days ago,' the man
explained, 'Not many people know we're here, so
things haven't had a chance to get going yet.'

Laughter echoed throughout the play centre as a
boy chased a girl from one area to another.

'Now,' the man said, 'can I have your children's
names, please?'

'Finlay!' Finlay said, grinning.

Thomas said nothing, so Mrs Tinkler said, 'And
Thomas.'

The man made a note of this in a logbook, plus the
time they'd entered.

'And how long will you be staying?' the man
asked.

'Just an hour,' Mrs Tinkler said.

'Okay,' the man said, making another entry in the
logbook. 'That's seven pounds. If you change your
minds and decide you want to stay longer, it's only a

pound extra.'

'We may decide to do that,' Mrs Tinkler said, handing over a ten pound note.

The man gave her some change, then buzzed the entry gate so they could enter.

'Have an exciting time,' the man said. He focused his attention on Thomas. 'Especially you, my little friend. Oh yes yes *yes*.'

Mr and Mrs Tinkler grabbed a table in the corner.

'Right, I'm parched so I'm going to get a cup of tea,' Mr Tinkler said. He asked Mrs Tinkler if she wanted one.

'Yes, please,' she replied. 'And I'll have a slice of chocolate cake, if there's any going. Anything will do, otherwise.'

'Do you pair want anything?' Mr Tinkler asked the boys.

Daft question – of course they did.

'Can I have a packet of crisps and a can of coke, please?' Finlay said.

'Not a problem,' Mr Tinkler said.

Thomas said, 'Can I have ... erm, a bar of chocolate and a coke, please?'

'Okey-doke,' Mr Tinkler said.

'Wouldn't you like something a little more healthy?' Mrs Tinkler said to her sons. 'Some fruit and a nice drink of juice would be better.'

'You can't lecture them about healthy eating when you're having chocolate cake,' Mr Tinkler pointed out.

10

'Good point,' Mrs Tinkler said.

Finlay kicked his trainers off and Thomas followed suit, less enthusiastically.

Then Finlay took off at pace, heading towards the section that housed the biggest slide.

'What are you waiting for?' Mrs Tinkler said to Thomas, shooing him away. 'Go on, get after him.'

Rolling his eyes, he took off after his brother, walking slowly.

By the time Thomas reached the play area, Finlay was already coming down the slide, 'Woo-*hoo!*' he screeched with his arms in the air. He slid to a stop in front of Thomas.

'I don't think that much has changed,' Thomas said. 'They've just added the castle bit to the front of the main play frame, but everything else is the same. There's nothing else that's new, as far as I can see.'

'Not true,' Finlay said, getting up. 'At least one other thing has changed. Come on, I'll show you.'

Finlay led him back into the main play frame. They passed through the ball pool area and Thomas couldn't resist throwing one at Finlay, which pinged off the back of his head.

'*Hey!*' Finlay said, wheeling around and returning fire.

A ball hit Thomas in the face and he collapsed dramatically, pretending to be dead. And then Finlay was on top of him, wrestling him, trying to bury him beneath the balls. After a few seconds, Thomas turned the tables and began tickling his brother.

'*Stop ... it!*' Finlay said through fits of laughter.

But Thomas carried on tickling.

'*Stop ... IT!*' Finlay begged, kicking out with his legs.

And then Thomas did. 'Go on then, squirt; show me this new thing.'

Getting up and making his way out of the ball pool, Finlay couldn't resist throwing one last ball at Thomas before exiting.

'Right, that's it,' Thomas said, taking off after him.

By the time he caught him, Finlay had reached the new addition that he wanted to show his brother. Standing on a long, thin beam, holding a foam battle axe, Finlay grinned and beckoned Thomas to join him.

'*Wicked!*' Thomas said, grabbing another axe and positioning himself on the beam in front of Finlay. 'You're for it now, little knight.'

'Go easy on me,' Finlay said, readying himself. 'I'm smaller than you, remember.'

'You want me to *let* you win? That wouldn't really be winning, would it?'

'Just go easy, yeah.'

'Okay.'

He jabbed the axe towards Finlay's midsection and Finlay parried it away with a defensive swipe.

'The Force is strong in this one,' Thomas said.

He was about to attack again, but Finlay beat him

to it, surprising him with a jab of his own. This caught Thomas by surprise, knocking him off the beam. He fell to his left and went sprawling.

'Yay, I win!' Finlay declared.

'Hey I wasn't ready!' Thomas said, getting back to his feet.

He went to stand back on the beam, ready to show Finlay who was boss, but then two other kids appeared: a boy and a girl. Thomas recognised them from earlier. The boy had been chasing the girl, their laughter echoing throughout the place. Now they wanted to have a go on the beam in a winner stays on contest.

'I'm the winner at the moment,' Finlay said, 'because I just knocked him off.'

'Only because I wasn't ready,' Thomas said indignantly.

'He's the same size as me,' the girl said, nodding towards Finlay, 'so can I have a go against him?'

'I suppose so,' Thomas said, handing her the axe and standing aside.

The girl mounted the beam. She flicked her blonde hair away from her shoulders, then announced she was ready.

Not wasting a second, Finlay brought his axe around in whooping arc. Unfortunately for him, the girl saw it coming and leant backwards, avoiding the blow. Finlay lost his balance, fell off the beam and dropped the axe.

'Ha-hah, I win!' the girl said, celebrating. 'And I didn't even have to hit you.'

Thomas couldn't help but find this funny.

The boy, who had ginger hair and freckles, stepped forwards. 'Looks like it's my go.' He picked up the axe and mounted the beam. 'You're not beating me, sis.'

'We'll see about that,' she said with grim determination.

The boy struck first, catching her in the tummy. She let out a gasp of surprise, but she kept her balance. The boy rained down blows, which she parried away. Thomas was just beginning to think that she might stand a chance of winning when the boy caught her with a clip to the side of the head. At first, she didn't look like she would fall. She lowered her weight, steadying herself. But then her foot slid and she fell to the mat, letting out a surprised 'Oomph!' as she went sprawling.

'I'm the champion!' the boy declared. 'No one can beat me!'

'We'll see about that,' Thomas said, picking up the axe and taking his place on the beam. 'So you can beat a little girl. Let's see how you handle someone your own size.'

The boy looked Thomas up and down, not impressed by what he was seeing. 'You think you can beat me?' He nodded towards Finlay. 'You couldn't even beat him and he's no bigger than my sister.'

Thomas didn't respond. He just stood on the beam,

axe in hand, ready.

'Please knock my brother off,' the girl said. 'His head will be so big he won't be able to get it through the door if he wins.'

The boys sized each other up.

Then Thomas faked an attack, jabbing his axe out with blurring speed. The boy managed no more than a flinch in response.

'Think you're clever, do you?' the boy said. 'We'll see who's smiling at the end.'

He faked his own jab, but Thomas was ready for this and had anticipated the move. He ducked and whacked the boy on the side of the leg as hard as he could, causing him to wobble. The boy flailed about with his hands in the air, trying to keep his balance. And that's when Thomas – sporting a big, toothy grin – knocked him off the beam. The boy crashed to his side, against the padded wall.

His sister let out a cry of jubilation.

'Ella, you're supposed to be on my side,' the boy said. 'You're my sister, remember.'

'I would be on your side,' she said, 'if you weren't being such a fat head. Honestly, Brady, sometimes you're just embarrassing.'

'I am not being a fat head!' Brady said, standing up. 'And I'm not embarrassing, either.'

'Yes you are,' Ella said.

'Am not!' Brady replied, looking tearful.

'Yes you are.'

'Am *not!*'

'You are!'

'Am *NOT!*'

'Whoa,' Thomas said, holding up a hand, trying to calm things. 'O-kay, I think me and my brother are going to move on now.' He tossed his axe aside and went to walk away, motioning Finlay to follow him.

Brady said, 'You can't go yet. You need to give me a chance to win you back.'

'I would do,' Thomas said, 'but we didn't come here to listen to bickering.'

'We hear enough of that at home,' Finlay said, 'without hearing it at the play centre.'

'That's a fair enough comment,' Brady conceded. 'So ... okay, maybe I was being a bit big-headed. I still think I deserve a re-match, though.'

His sister spoke up. 'Maybe you can have a rematch, but it's his go now,' Ella said, gesturing towards Finlay.

'Okay,' Thomas said, picking up the axe and mounting the beam again, 'we'll have a few more goes, but then I want to move on to another bit to see if anything else has changed here.'

And so on and on the contest went. Thomas got two wins in a row, knocking both Finlay and Ella off with ease. Stepping up for the re-match, Brady looked even more determined to win the second encounter with Thomas. But, as things turned out, it ended up as a draw. Both boys struck each other at the same time and both lost their balance, then fell from the beam.

'Can we go to another part now?' Finlay said. 'I'm getting tired of this.'

Brady seemed happy that he'd battled his way to a draw, so he nodded in agreement, as did the others.

'Last one down the big slide is a great big poo-poo head!' Ella said, running away and making her way up the padded steps before anyone else could even think about moving.

'I'm not being a poo-poo head,' Finlay said, taking off after her

Shrugging, Brady followed suit, leaving just Thomas.

'Looks like I'm going to be the poo-poo head,' he said, setting off.

By the time he got to the top, Finlay had already gone down the wide slide and was waiting at the bottom. Brady and Ella Woo-hoo-ed! as they went down together. This left just Thomas, who was about to join them when something caught his eye. He forgot about the slide and made his way towards a doorway, which was in an alcove at the end of the run.

'That wasn't there before,' he said. He stared blankly at the door, which had golden writing etched into it:

Sometimes a bridge will span my width and sometimes it will not. Sometimes I can be full of water and sometimes I am not. If you tumble from the walls and I'm filled with water, I'll break your fall with a splash. What am I?

'No idea,' Thomas said, shaking his head.

'You are now a poo-poo head,' Finlay said, appearing next to him. 'Why didn't you follow us down the slide?'

Thomas didn't respond. He was still busy trying to work out what the writing meant.

'I'm going back to Mum and Dad in a minute, so I can scoff my crisps,' Finlay said. 'Are you coming?'

'Oh here you are,' Brady said as he and his sister joined them. 'What are you up to, you pair?'

Ella read the writing out loud. 'That's a riddle,' she said. 'We did some in class last week, so I know a riddle when I see one.'

'You're right,' Thomas said, 'it is a riddle – but what does it mean?' He clicked his fingers together as he gave it some thought. 'The theme of this place is now medieval, so I bet it's something to do with that. I'm useless at this sort of thing.'

'Sometimes a bridge will span my width and sometimes it will not,' Finlay said, sounding confused.

'Perhaps it's referring to a river,' Thomas suggested. 'Some rivers have bridges that go up and down to let boats pass.'

The others looked unconvinced.

Ella read the next part, looking equally confused: 'Sometimes I can be full of water and sometimes I am not.' She mulled things over for a few seconds. 'What about a bath? Sometimes a bath is full of water and sometimes it isn't.'

'Nice try, sis,' Brady said. 'But the answer needs to fit with the rest of the riddle.'

Thomas read the final part: 'If you fall from the walls and I'm filled with water, I'll break your fall with a splash.'

'Castles have walls and they're medieval,' Finlay said. 'So maybe it's something to do with a castle.'

'That's it!' Brady said. 'The answer is a moat! A drawbridge spans its width when it's down. Some moats have water in them and some don't. And if you fell from the castle walls, you'd make a splash when you hit the water. So that's the answer: a *moat!*'

Click!

The door opened slightly, making everyone jump.

'Uh-oh, what's this?' Brady said, taking a step back.

'Only one way to find out,' Thomas said. He pushed the door open. And then a look of amazement slowly spread across his face, because he couldn't believe what he was seeing: a huge castle.

CHAPTER TWO

(the coolest castle ever)

Stepping through the doorway, with the others filing in behind him, Thomas looked up at the castle, which was set in a cavernous room. It had four towers, like the one at the front of the play frame. But instead of being just a frontage, this appeared to be a full-blown castle: complete with a drawbridge and moat.

'Wow,' Brady said. 'How cool is that?'

'*Seriously* cool,' Finlay said in awe.

'Seriously, *seriously*, cool,' Thomas said.

But Ella was a little more cautious. 'Erm,' she said. 'Don't you think this a little weird? I mean, we got in here because we solved a riddle. And look at that castle – it's huge and it looks almost real.'

'It's not a real one,' Brady said. 'The walls are rubber.'

'I didn't say it was real,' Ella replied. 'I said that it looks *almost* real.'

'I wonder if we can get inside,' Finlay said.

'The drawbridge is up, so I don't think so,' Thomas said.

Something caught his eye. At the far end of the room was a tall wall that stretched from one side to the other, butting up against the rear of the castle.

'Wonder what's behind there?' Brady said.

'Doesn't look like there's any way to get past it,' Thomas said, setting off across the padded floor, towards the castle. As he got closer, he noticed that the moat was filled with plastic balls, like the ones in the ball pool. 'Come on, you lot – what are you waiting for?'

Finlay and Brady followed after him. Ella stayed where she was, though.

'I'm going back into the normal play area,' she said, 'because this is a little too odd for my liking, thank you very much.'

She turned to leave, but the door closed shut with a

snap. She tried to open it, but there was no handle for her to pull and she couldn't prise it open at the edges with her fingers.

Pushing her aside, Brady tried some prising of his own and didn't have any luck either.

'Oh, great!' Ella said, throwing her hands up in the air. 'Now we're trapped!'

She banged on the door, hoping to attract someone's attention. 'Help!' she yelled. 'Hello! We're locked in here! Somebody help! Please let us out!' She continued banging her fists on the door and calling for help, until Thomas put a hand on her shoulder.

'I don't think anyone can hear you,' he said.

'We need to get out of here,' replied Ella, looking wild-eyed and panicky.

'Calm down,' her brother said to her. 'Even if we are locked in here, there's no reason to have a meltdown. As soon as our parents realise we're missing, they'll come looking for us. It's only a matter of time before we're found.'

Both Thomas and Finlay tried their hand at opening the door, without success.

So Thomas turned his attention back to the castle. As he got closer, he realised that something was written on the drawbridge, etched out in golden writing: another riddle.

'That wasn't there when I looked before,' he mumbled, edging as close as he could so he could read what it said:

I wear a suit and move slowly, but I'm well protected. You can be my squire if you call me sir, help me put on my suit and tend my other needs. My weapons of choice are the lance and the sword (and a mace with some spikes makes my enemies wish they'd never been born). What am I?

Brady appeared at Thomas's side. 'Another riddle,' Brady said. 'That's all we need. This just keeps getting weirder and weirder.' He read it. 'Any idea what it means? My dad wears a suit. Maybe that's the answer.'

His words sailed past Thomas, who was desperately trying to think of the proper answer to the riddle. He was finding it hard to concentrate though, because Ella had resumed banging on the door, demanding to be let out.

'Can you *please* tell your sister to stop making all that noise,' Thomas moaned. 'It really isn't helping.'

Sloping away, Brady went to calm Ella. He pulled her to one side and began talking to her in a soothing tone.

Finlay joined Thomas by the drawbridge. He followed Thomas's sightline and then read the riddle. 'Well that's a lot easier than the first one,' he said. 'Not much of a challenge at all.'

'Really?' Thomas said. 'You've figured it out?'

'Yes,' Finlay replied proudly. 'The answer is a knight. The lance gave it away for me. I don't know of anyone other than a knight who'd carry a lance. And it fits in with the rest of the riddle. You'd be well protected and slow if you were wearing a "suit" of armour. I remember Mrs Emerson at school teaching us about squires and how they tended to a knight's needs. And, back in medieval times, knights were always referred to as sirs.'

A loud clanking sound got everyone's attention. Then the drawbridge began to lower.

'You did it!' Thomas said to Finlay. 'Nice one.'

Finlay danced a little jig in celebration.

When the drawbridge had finished lowering, Thomas and Finlay moved closer to see what was beyond the archway that'd been revealed.

'There's a courtyard,' Thomas said. 'Come on, let's go and have a look.'

'Hey, wait up you pair!' Brady said. 'You can't just leave us in here.'

'Come with us, then,' Thomas said.

'I'm not going in there,' Ella replied, staying rooted. 'The best thing we can do is stay here. It's the *sensible* thing to do. When my parents come looking for me, I want to be by this door, so I can hear them.'

'Can you hear anything on the other side of the door now?' Brady asked her.

She put her ear against it, then shook her head. 'No.'

'Neither can I,' Brady said. 'But we should be able to. If we can't hear anything through that door, then that means that anyone on the other side won't be able to hear us either.'

Ella took a few seconds to process this, and then she burst into tears.

Kneeling before her, Brady gave her a hug and said, 'It's okay, sis; I'm here with you, so you're safe.'

'I'm *scared*,' she sobbed. 'I don't like being locked in here – I want out out *out!*'

'I'll get us out,' Brady said.

He moved Ella out of the way, then lined himself up with the door. He ran at it and kicked it as hard as he could. It didn't do any good, though. The door didn't budge an inch. He tried two more kicks before deciding that another approach might be a good idea.

'Perhaps if all pushed at the same time,' he suggested, 'then that might do the trick.'

'It won't,' Thomas said. 'You're wasting your time.'

'Maybe I am,' Brady responded. 'But it's got to be better to keep trying than admit defeat.'

Ella's little shoulders hitched up and down as she

continued to sob.

'Fine,' Thomas said, 'if it'll make you happy.'

He and Finlay joined Brady by the door and the three of them pushed as hard as they could – to no avail.

'Told you we'd be wasting our time,' Thomas said.

Brady said, 'You're not trying hard enough. We need to *really* give it some welly. Let's have another go.'

'I was pushing as hard as I could,' Thomas said.

'And so was I,' Finlay added.

'Just one more go,' Brady said. 'Push like your lives depend on it.'

'Okay,' Thomas said, almost certain that the outcome would be the same.

And, as it turned out, the outcome was the same. But neither Brady nor his sister would admit defeat.

'Persistence will pay off,' he said. 'We just need to keep at it.'

'*You* can keep at it,' Thomas said, walking away. 'Me and my brother aren't wasting anymore time on this. We're going into the castle, because I think that's the only way we're going to get out of here.'

'Why do you say that?' Brady said. 'Why would you think that?'

Thomas stopped and explained. 'Look,' he said taking a few seconds to mull over how best to convey the conclusions he'd drawn, 'it's pretty obvious what's going on, if you think about it. We found a door with a mysterious riddle written on it. We solved it and were let through. Then we found ourselves in this place. And then we've had to solve another riddle to bring down the drawbridge. That's two challenges we've faced so far, and my guess is that there are other challenges waiting for us inside that castle. I don't think we'll be able to get out of here without passing those challenges.'

'My brother doesn't normally talk much sense,' Finlay said, 'but I think he is now.'

'What do you mean I don't normally talk sense?' Thomas said, giving his brother a stern look.

Finlay just shrugged and smiled at him.

'Okay,' Thomas said, addressing Brady and his sister, 'we don't know if that drawbridge will go back up. And if it does, we don't know whether we'll be able to get it down again. Finlay and me are going to wait here another five minutes to see if anything happens. If the drawbridge does start rising, we'll have to make a run for it.'

He paced back and forth, counting in his head. During this time Ella kept her vigil by the door, banging on it intermittently with her fist and calling for help. Brady stood with her, looking lost and confused. Finlay, meanwhile, was wandering up and down the side of the castle, taking a keen interest in it.

When Thomas was sure that the five minutes had passed, he said to Brady and Ella, 'Are you pair coming with us or not?'

Brady looked at Ella and she shook her head.

'If my sister won't go inside, then I'm not going in either,' he said. 'I can't leave her on her own.'

'Change your mind and you know where we'll be,' Thomas said, beckoning Finlay to follow him.

Finlay scurried after him. 'We might need them,' he said. 'You know what Dad says about two heads being better than one. Well, four heads are better than two, and we'll stand a better chance of solving any other riddles if we've got them with us.'

'I know that,' Thomas responded. 'But if they won't come, we can't make them.'

Stopping in front of the drawbridge, Thomas looked up at the castle, then down at his brother, who was standing by his side. 'Are you ready for this, Finlay?' Thomas asked him. 'Ready to see what's inside?'

'I suppose so,' he said, looking more than a little anxious. 'About as ready as I'll ever be. There's really no other option, is there? How long do you think it'll be before the other two realise that?'

'I don't know. Ten minutes. An hour. Who knows?'

As Thomas and Finlay walked across the drawbridge, their feet clattering across the plastic boards, Thomas cast one last glance towards the other two. Brady was banging on the door again, pounding away with his fist while his sister watched him. Her eyes were still glazed from crying. Her shoulders were still hitching up and down in jittery bursts.

Thomas felt like he was abandoning her and Brady, but there was no other option, as far as he could see. *If we find a way out, we'll come back and find you,* Thomas thought. *We'll tell your parents, our parents, anyone and everyone that'll listen, and then we'll come back and get you.*

And so into the courtyard he and Finlay went, taking in their surroundings. The floor was made from spongy cobblestones, which made Thomas feel like he was walking on air. Up high, arched windows lined the walls. Thomas counted four doorways: three at ground level and one at the top of a stairway to his left. A note tacked to the wall at the far end caught Thomas's eye. Darting towards it, he snatched it up and read it out loud.

Greetings and salutations,

Ahead of you are three main challenges to test your wit and wares. They're marked by a giant **X**, so you'll know just when and where. Win two out of three and you'll be happy – ho, ho. Back home you'll go, telling stories of bravado. Lose on the other hand and things could get heated. You'll disappear in the blink of an eye as if you've been deleted.

Best of luck and have a jolly good day.

J.T.

'J.T.?' Finlay said. 'Who's J.T.?'

Thomas shrugged. 'No idea. Did the guy behind the counter mention his name?'

'I don't think so. I'm pretty sure he didn't.'

'I bet it is him. Who else could it be?'

This time Finlay shrugged. 'I dunno. But we need to show this note to the others. I'm sure they'll come with us if we do.'

Before Thomas could reply, the drawbridge began to go back up.

'If we're going to try and get back to them, we better do it now,' Finlay said.

By the time they'd made their way back across the courtyard, the drawbridge had already been raised halfway.

'If we run up it, maybe we'll be able to jump across to the other side of the moat,' Finlay suggested.

'Yes,' Thomas replied. 'But then we might not be able to get back in.'

Just before it got to its fully-raised position, Thomas heard Brady shout something, but Thomas couldn't make out what he'd said.

And then - *clank!* - that was it.

No going back now.

Finlay looked at Thomas, who knew what he must be thinking.

'You feel trapped now, don't you?' Thomas said.

Finlay nodded solemnly.

'Doing whatever needs to be done in here is the

only way we're going to get out of this place,' Thomas said. He held the note up. 'And at least we know what we're doing now – kind of. Three main challenges: whatever they are. That's what stands between us and getting back to Mum and Dad.'

'Three "main" challenges. Does that mean there will be others?'

'I wondered when you were going to pick up on that. It certainly sounds like there could be.' Thomas put his hands on his brother's shoulders and crouched down slightly so he was on the same eye level. 'But whatever's coming our way, we'll face it together. We'll *beat* it together. We can do this. Yeah?'

Finlay gave him a nod. 'Yeah.'

They could hear Brady and Ella shouting outside, but they couldn't make out what they were saying.

'Hey, we've found a note!' Finlay yelled up towards the ceiling above the castle. 'We've found a note!'

'You're wasting your breath,' Thomas said. 'If we can't understand what they're saying, then they won't be able to understand what we're saying.'

Realising that his brother was right, Finlay turned his attention towards the four doors in the courtyard. 'Which one should we go through?'

'Not sure. Only one way to find out.'

Thomas tried the two to the right, but they were both locked. Finlay tried the one remaining ground level door, which was on the other side of the courtyard, but that was locked as well.

'It must be that one then,' Finlay said, pointing to the door at the top of the stairs.

Thomas pocketed the note.

Taking the steps two at a time, he reached the top, then tried the door.

'This one's locked as well,' he said.

'Oh. So what do we do now then?'

Thomas shrugged. 'Your guess is as good as mine.'

He could see the windows better from this elevated position. Just for a second - a *split* second - he thought he caught a glimpse of movement in one of them.

'What's wrong?' Finlay said, trying to follow his gaze. 'What have you seen?'

Thomas looked again, but he couldn't see anything untoward. *Perhaps it was just a shadow*, he thought. *Or my imagination getting the better of me.*

'Nothing,' he replied. 'I didn't see anything.'

Luka joined Finlay at the bottom of the steps and they began checking the ground level doors again, just to make sure they were locked.

When they'd finished and established that they all were, Thomas said, 'You're going to ask me what we should do now, aren't you?'

'No, I'm not,' Finlay replied, motioning towards something in the centre of the courtyard.

'Where did they come from? They weren't there when we came in.'

Finlay shrugged. 'They just appeared. One second

there was nothing there … and then there was.'

Scrambling across the courtyard, Thomas went to see the big pile of soft play building blocks that'd materialised out of thin air.

'I wonder what we're supposed to do with this lot,' he said.

Finlay had the answer. 'The stairway has disappeared, so I'm guessing that we need to build a new one with these.'

'What, so we can make our way back up to that locked door? What would be the point of that?'

Click!

They both looked towards the door, realising that it'd been unlocked.

'Oh, well, at least we know what we're supposed to be doing now,' Finlay said. 'This could be kind of fun.'

'It would be if we weren't on a time limit.' Thomas pointed to a digital clock that'd materialised on the far wall. It was counting down from three minutes.

177 seconds ... 176 ... 175 ...

'What do you think will happen if it reaches zero and we haven't got through the door?'

'I don't want to find out,' Thomas said, guessing that it would not be something good. 'Let's get building.'

Picking up blocks, both boys moved them to near where the original stairway had been.

When they'd transferred enough to get things started, Thomas said, 'Okay, I'll get building while you bring the rest of the blocks over here.'

'Okay.' Finlay scurried back and forth, moving them as fast as he could.

Meanwhile, Thomas began stacking them on top of each other. He created a wide base so his construction would be stable, and then he worked his way up from there, casting occasional glances towards the clock.

... 150 ... 149 ... 148 ...

'Don't slow down,' Thomas said, 'keep shifting those blocks.'

'I'm not slowing down!'

'I didn't say you were; I just want to make sure you keep the pace.'

'Don't you worry about what I'm doing – you just keep piling those blocks up.'

Higher and higher the construction went ...

... 130 ... 129 ... 128 ...

When Finlay had finished moving all the blocks, he called up to Thomas, who was by now building the third level: 'Do you want me to help you now?'

'Yes, you can pass me the blocks up. The higher I get, the slower I'm going. I have to keep coming back to the bottom to get more blocks and I can only carry one at a time.'

Finlay got busy again. 'How many more levels do you think we'll need to build?'

'About another five, I think.'

'*Five?* Do you think we'll need that many?'

'Yes, that's why I just said so. We'll be able to work

faster if you stop talking and concentrate on what we're doing, you know.'

... 111 ... 110 ... 109 ...

Nearly half the time had elapsed and they'd only built half their make-shift staircase. With the more difficult part still to construct, Thomas knew they needed to up the pace if they wanted to stand any chance of finishing by the time the clock reached zero.

But then they both stopped as a metallic clanking noise echoed throughout the courtyard. The boys looked towards the drawbridge, hopeful that it was being lowered again, hopeful that Brady and Ella would be joining them ...

No such luck.

'What was that noise?' Finlay asked.

'I don't know and I don't want to find out. Let's keep working.'

With an ever-growing sense of unease, Thomas resumed stacking blocks.

... 82 ... 81 ... 80 ...

By the time they'd finished the fourth level, Thomas's arms were beginning to ache. And he wasn't the only one who was suffering: Finlay's arms were aching, and his legs were, too. He'd slowed so much that Thomas now had to wait for him to bring up each block.

'I know it's hurting,' Thomas said, 'but you need to push through the pain. Try and think of something else, so you can distract your mind away from the discomfort.'

Stopping abruptly, Finlay said, 'We need to swap around. You bring the blocks up and I'll stack them, otherwise we'll never complete this in time.'

'But you'll stack them wrong or something, then I'll end up having to try and sort it out. We won't have time for that before the clock runs down.'

'I may be seven years old, but I'm not stupid, Thomas; I know the pile needs to be wide at the bottom and gradually get narrower as it gets higher. I can see what you're doing.'

Thomas threw his hands up in the air. 'Okay, whatever, fine – but if you mess this up, then heaven only knows what'll happen.'

The metallic clanking noise rang out in the courtyard, giving them some indication.

What is *that noise?* Thomas thought.

... 64 ... 63 ... 62 ...

Exchanging concerned looks with each other, the boys swapped positions and set to work. With a fresh burst of enthusiastic energy, Thomas made sure Finlay didn't waste a second waiting around to be supplied with blocks. And, to Thomas's pleasant surprise, Finlay was stacking them well, too: just as Thomas would have done himself.

'We should have done it this way to begin with,' Thomas said, quite happy to admit that he'd underestimated his brother's make-shift staircase building abilities.

Finlay slotted a block in place. 'Yes,' he agreed with a twinkle in his eyes, 'we should have.'

... 48 ... 47 ... 46 ...

'Forty-six seconds to build three more levels,' Thomas said. 'And the last one will only need four on it.'

'Eezy peezy.'

It should have been eezy peezy, and it would have been ... if Thomas hadn't lost his footing, then tumbled all the way to the bottom. He hit the padded cobblestones with a thud, which drove the wind out of him.

'Are you all right?' Finlay said, looking on with concern.

He went to go to his brother, so Thomas held up a hand. 'No, stay there – I'm okay.'

Feeling lucky that he'd had a soft landing, Thomas got to his feet. Knowing that there would now be not a second to waste, he picked up a block and began climbing back up towards Finlay.

... 35 ... 34 ... 33 ...

'Are you sure you're all right?' Finlay asked again. 'You don't look too good.'

'I'm just a bit winded, that's all.'

Clank! Clank! Clank!

'What is that noise?' Finlay said.

'Whatever it is, it's getting louder, which can't be good.'

After handing Finlay another block, Thomas made

his way back to the bottom and resumed what he was doing. He still felt winded, but he was determined that it wouldn't slow him down. If they were to stand any chance of completing the staircase, he *couldn't* let it slow him. Thomas tried carrying two blocks at a time, but he couldn't manage it.

'You can't carry any more than one, because they're too big,' Finlay said.

'I thought it was worth a try!'

.... 22 ... 21 ... 20 ...

Up and down Thomas went – up and down, all the time casting glances towards the clock. *We're not going to do it*, he thought as the seconds ticked away. *Whatever is making that clanking noise is going to appear soon and it's going to get us!*

'Come on, keep up the pace,' Finlay said. 'We only need to do the top section now. Just four more and that'll do it.'

This spurred Thomas on. But he knew there wasn't enough time left to shift another four blocks. 'Two will have to be enough,' he explained to Finlay.

'The top level won't be very stable. We'll have to be careful, otherwise we could fall.'

'We *will* be careful.'

Thomas handed Finlay the second to last block.

... 11 ... 10 ... 9 ...

'Oh no, only eight seconds left!' Thomas said as he once more darted off down the pile of blocks and retrieved another.

On the way back up he slipped and almost lost his footing again. Had he have fallen, then that would have been it – game over.

At the bottom, he grabbed the last block and scrambled back up to the top of their newly-built staircase. He handed it to Finlay, who didn't waste any time. He placed it in position, then stood on the top level so he could reach the door handle.

As he did so, Thomas cast one last glance towards the clock as it ran down towards zero.

... 4 ... 3 ... 2 ...

It isn't going to open, he thought dismally. *We've built this staircase for nothing and it isn't going to open.* But it did.

The clock hit zero, and a buzzer sounded.

Clank! CLANK! CLANK!

'Come on,' Finlay said, 'what are you waiting for?'

Thomas turned and saw that his brother was holding his hand out to him. He had opened the door and was now standing in the doorway, beckoning him to come through.

As Finlay had predicted, the two blocks that formed the top layer weren't as sturdy as four would have been. He climbed onto one and it tilted towards him slightly.

'Careful,' Finlay warned, 'or you'll go tumbling again.'

Shifting his weight forwards, Thomas climbed up and took his brother's hand.

CLANK! CLANK! CLANK!
Click!

'What was that last noise?' Finlay asked.

'Sounded like a door being unlocked.'

Thomas was right. Across the courtyard, the one nearest them began to open.

Just before he exited the courtyard, he caught sight of a foot emerging through the doorway: a foot that was clad in what looked like plastic armour.

Both boys breathed sighs of relief as Finlay closed the door they'd just disappeared through.

'Did you see what was making that clanking noise?' Finlay asked. 'Did you get a glimpse?'

Thomas told him what he'd seen. 'I think that foot belongs to a knight.' Then he bent over and put his hands on his knees, so he could catch his breath.

'A knight? What do you mean? Like, as in a *real* knight?'

'They're the only ones I can think of that wear armour, and we are in a castle, after all.'

'Did you see if he was carrying any weapons? A sword or an axe or something?'

'Like I said, I just glimpsed a foot – covered in armour. *Plastic* armour.'

'What do you think he'd have done to us if we hadn't made it through to here in time?'

'Let's not try and think about that, yeah.'

'Are we safe in here? What if he climbs up the tower of blocks we built and comes after us?'

'He'd do well to climb anything wearing a suit of armour (even one made of plastic). I think we're okay in here.'

'Normally I'd agree with you, but with this strange stuff that's been happening ...'

'Best get moving, then, hadn't we?'

They went to move off, but Finlay said, 'D'you think that was one of the main challenges we just completed? It seemed difficult enough to be a "main" challenge.'

'Did you see an X anywhere in that courtyard?'

'No.'

'Neither did I.'

'Maybe we missed it.'

'Somehow, I don't think we did.'

'Oh,' Finlay said, looking concerned. 'But if that was one of the lesser challenges, what will the main ones be like? That one was hard enough!'

'We got through it. That's all that counts. And we'll get through whatever's coming next.'

Turning their attention to the corridor they were now standing in, the boys noticed the next obstacle they would have to negotiate: a narrow beam that ran from one end to the other. About five feet beneath the beam was an area full of plastic balls. Beyond this, at the far end of the corridor, was a netted climbing rope grid, which led up to another level.

'I don't see an X,' Finlay said.

'Me neither.'

'This looks easy enough, though. Even if we fall off, we'll have a soft landing.'

'I doubt it's going to be that easy.'

As it turned out, Thomas was right. From below the balls came a rustling sound, then some of them began moving up and down.

'What's that?' Finlay asked, edging away.

A sliver of gooseflesh ran up Thomas's arms. 'Please stop asking me lots of questions,' he said. 'It's *really* getting on my nerves now. I don't know what it is, but I'm pretty certain it's not going to be good for us. How's your balance?'

'I did okay on the beam earlier, in the other part of this play centre, and you did even better.'

'That was just standing still on one. We've got to walk across this one, and it's quite a long way. As long as we remain calm, we should be all right. Assuming there are no other dangers in here, of course.'

As if on cue, down both sides of the room along its length, small cupboard holes opened and plastic Nerf crossbows appeared from within each.

'I had to open my big mouth,' Thomas said with dismay.

'They're Nerf Dreadbolts. I wanted one of those last Christmas, but Mum said I couldn't have one.'

'That's because you've got about twenty Nerf guns already.'

'Yes but I haven't got a crossbow.'

'At least we're not being timed for this challenge.'

'Don't say that. That's not a clever thing to say, now, is it?'

Finlay slapped a hand over his mouth, then pretended to zip his lips shut. 'Maybe it'd be best if I just didn't talk from now on,' he said.

'That's not a bad suggestion.' Thomas gave things some thought. 'Look, if those crossbows fire regular arrows, we should be okay. I know they can hurt if they hit you at close range, but they won't hit us hard enough to knock us off. We just need to ignore them and concentrate on not losing our balance.'

'*If* they fire regular arrows at regular power. That's a *very* iffy if, given what's happened to us in the last twenty minutes or so.'

'Got any better suggestions?'

Finlay glanced towards the door they'd just come through.

'That knight is probably still out there. You can take a look if you like, but who knows what else might be out there now. At least in here we know what we're up against and what needs to be done.'

'We don't know what we're up against, though, do we? We don't know what's beneath those balls.'

The balls moved up and down again.

'What if it's a creature with long tentacles? What if, while we're walking across, it reaches up, grabs us and drags us down? What if it's an alligator or a crocodile? Or Piranha (they're small but deadly, you know!). What if it's a ...'

'Oh quit it with the what-ifs, will you,' Thomas hissed, cutting him off. 'We have no way of knowing and all this guesswork is just making me more hesitant to cross. And besides, that's a ball pool down there, or haven't you noticed? Alligators and crocs and Piranha live in water, *not* pools of balls.'

'Not normally, but ...'

Thomas put a hand over his brother's mouth. 'I'd gag you if I could.'

Shrugging him off, Finlay said, 'So ... who's going first?'

'I am.'

Finlay offered no protest.

Thomas stepped forwards and lined himself up with the beam. He recalled the time he had visited the circus with his parents. One of the acts had balanced on a ball with her hands held out at her sides. This, his mother had told him, was so the woman would have better stability. Adopting the same technique now, Thomas held his hands out at his sides, then mounted the beam.

Fast or slow, he wondered. *Should I bolt across or take my time?* "Mistakes happen when people rush," Mrs Tinkler had once said to Thomas when he was doing his homework. So he decided that having momentum would be a good thing, but that having too much momentum would probably not be good.

'Are you going, then, or what?' Finlay asked.

'Yes, I *am*,' Thomas said, setting off.

As he took his first steps, he heard a clicking sound and assumed it was the Dreadbolts being loaded. *Great*, he thought, *I'm about to get blasted.* He passed the first one and a foam-tipped arrow pinged off the side of his head.

'*Oww!*' he said, stopping and wincing.

'Try and keep moving.'

'That hurt more than I thought it would.'

'Now you can see why I want to get one.'

'If we can ever get out of this place then maybe you will.'

Still holding his hands out, Thomas pressed on, concentrating hard as he placed one foot in front of the other. The balls stirred beneath him, but he didn't stop to see if anything emerged. He was sure that Finlay would let him know if that were the case. *Bzzzz!* An arrow whizzed past him like an angry insect.

'You're doing well,' Finlay said encouragingly. 'You're nearly halfway already.'

Thomas kept moving ...

Thump! An arrow struck his shoulder. Not letting it faze him, he concentrated on the task ahead, keeping his cool.

He took two more hits from Nerf arrows.

And then that was it – he reached the other side.

'Yeah!' he said, raising a hand in celebration. 'Easy as can be.' He turned his attention to his brother, who did not look confident at all. 'Just take your time,

45

don't worry about anything other than getting over here. And if you get hit by something, ignore it. Focus on the beam.' Thomas was about to tell him to try to forget about whatever might be beneath the balls, but he didn't want to bring Finlay's attention to this.

Finlay, however, was looking down at the balls anyway, so Thomas knew what he was thinking.

'Come on,' Thomas said. 'You saw how I did it. All you have to do is copy me, yeah. You can do this, Finlay; I know you can.'

'Okay,' he said, steeling himself. 'Oooo-kay.'

'Don't think about how far you've got to go – just concentrate on the next step, and then the one after that, then the one after that ...'

'*Oooo*-kay,' Finlay said, moving onto the beam and advancing forwards.

He took four steps and nearly fell sideways. '*Whooo!*' he said, regaining his balance.

Beneath him, the balls moved up and down, up and down.

Then a Nerf arrow hit him in the ear.

'I can't make it all the way across,' Finlay said, panicking. 'I'm going back.'

'No, don't stop now. If you go back, you'll never get the courage up to try again.'

'But what if some tentacles reach up and grab me,' Finlay said, his voice quivering. He looked like he could burst in to tears any second.

Thomas beckoned him forwards. 'Look, just stay

calm. Concentrate on the beam and think of nothing else. Forget the arrows – like I said, they won't hit you anywhere near hard enough to knock you off. Take deep breathes: inhale, exhale ... inhale, exhale. It'll help. And keep your arms up. It really does help if you hold them out.'

Finlay put his arms out. He wobbled a bit, then steadied himself again.

'Deep breathes,' he said. 'Inhale ...' he breathed in, 'and exhale.' He breathed out.

'That's great. Now come to me.'

Tentatively, Finlay began moving forwards once more. The balls stirred below him, but this time he didn't stop. He put one foot in front of the other. With each step he took, his confidence grew. More arrows hit him and he didn't even flinch. As he passed halfway, Thomas gave him an encouraging smile.

'You're doing brill,' Thomas said smiling, curling his fingers over in a keep moving gesture.

'This is easy,' Finlay said.

'Don't get overconfident.'

Onwards Finlay pressed, picking up speed.

'And slow down. You're going too fast.'

'Easy as peezy,' Finlay said with a playful glint in his eyes.

'*Slow down!*' Thomas said. 'Oh crikey, why don't you ever listen to a word I say!'

An arrow pinged off the side of Finlay's head and he gave a chortle. 'Is that the best you can do?' he said, still advancing at pace. 'You could fire a hundred of those at me and it wouldn't do a thing.'

Only because you're used to me bombarding you with Nerf bullets, Thomas thought. 'Who are you talking to?' he asked his brother.

Stepping off the beam in front of him, Finlay said, 'Whoever created this place and locked us inside of here. The person who wrote the note: J.T.'

'The guy behind the counter?'

'The new owner of the play centre, yep. As you said, who else could it be?'

Whom else, indeed? Thomas hadn't given much thought as to why this had happened to him and his brother. *Perhaps he is right*, he thought. *Perhaps the strange man is the one behind all of this.* It seemed a logical enough assumption: the only one Thomas think of. *But why would that creepy old weirdo want to lock us in here and put these obstacles in front of us?* And then it came to him ...

'It's because I moaned that I was bored. *That's* why this is happening – because I moaned that I was bored and that guy is ... is ...'

'Punishing you? Punishing *us*?'

'No,' Thomas said, shaking his head. 'I don't think he's punishing us. I think he's trying to make things more interesting for us – more *exciting*.'

'Exciting!' Finlay said, pulling a strange face. 'That's not the word I would have used.'

'Me neither.'

'So ... this is all your fault? Because you turned up all moody and grouchy, we're now stuck in this castle.'

'I wouldn't exactly say it was my fault.'

'Whose fault is it then?'

'No ones. How was I supposed to know that this would happen?'

'Nothing's ever your fault, is it? Like when you accidently dropped my remote controlled car in the bath. That wasn't your fault, was it? Or when you spilt your drink all over my homework. That wasn't your fault, either. And what about the time when you ...'

'Okay, all right – you've made your point.' Thomas decided that a change of subject would be a good idea. 'You shouldn't have done that,' he said, gesturing towards the beam. 'You shouldn't have crossed so fast. It was a silly, reckless thing to do.'

'I didn't fall off.'

'That's not the point. Next time you might not be so lucky.'

'There was no luck involved,' Finlay said smugly. 'Just skill.'

'Well, you didn't look very skilful when you first started out. You were close to tears.'

Finlay shot his brother a reproachful look. 'Thanks for reminding me.'

A feeling of guilt washed over Thomas. 'I'm sorry,' he apologized, 'I shouldn't have said that.'

'It's okay,' Finlay replied, giving him a playful punch on the arm. 'I shouldn't have rushed across and I shouldn't have been boastful about it.'

The balls beneath the beam began moving again.

'Come on,' Finlay said, 'let's move on before a tentacle really does reach up and grab one of us.'

They focused their attention on the netted climbing rope grid.

'I hate these things,' Thomas said. 'I usually avoid them, because they hurt my feet.'

'There's no avoiding this one.'

Finlay went first, making short work of the rope grid. By the time he'd reached the top, Thomas was only halfway up.

'Uh-oh,' he heard Finlay say. 'Here we go again. More fun and games.'

'What is it?' Thomas asked. 'What's up there?'

Finlay looked down at him. 'Another locked door – and another riddle.'

'Great. That's just ... great.' Thomas's feet were really starting to hurt now, making him wince. 'Read it out loud, so I can be thinking about it as I'm climbing. It might take my mind off the pain.'

'A list of things you'll need for this game: two horses, two long spears, a tilt, two suits of armour, and a squire to help you put on the latter. Which game am I?'

Before Thomas could give this even a second's worth of thought, Finlay came up the answer: 'It's jousting. It *has* to be. The spears must be lances. Two horses, two suits of armour and a squire to help you put the latter on ... it all fits. Apart from the tilt thing. I've no idea what that might be.'

As Thomas neared the top, Finlay helped him up.

'That was not fun,' Thomas said, sitting down and rubbing the bottoms of his feet. He noticed that the door behind Finlay was now open. 'You know what, I've got to admit, you're pretty clever for your age, bro. We'd be stuck in this corridor for a long time if it was down to me to solve that riddle, I'm sure.'

'We wouldn't even be in this castle if it was down to you to figure these things out. Maybe I should have just kept my mouth shut. At least we wouldn't be stuck in this castle.'

'No. But we'd still be stuck outside of here, in that huge room. Brady solved the first riddle, so maybe we should blame him for all this happening.'

Even though I'm to blame, Thomas thought. *Why did I have to be such a misery guts?*

'Right,' he said, standing up, 'I suppose we better go and see what the next task has in store for us.'

'Each riddle so far has been a clue as to what's coming next. If it's something to do with jousting, then that sounds dangerous.'

'What I want to know is who's going to be jousting with who?'

The boys exchanged worried glances as they made their way through the door.

CHAPTER THREE

(fun & games in the saddle)

Entering another room, they looked around and saw that it had been bisected by a plastic barrier that ran its length. At each end of the barrier was a plastic horse. Facing each other, both were mounted on mechanical run-lines with a rubberised lance resting against each of them. Two digital displays mounted on top of each other on the far wall caught Thomas's eye. Both were blank. And beneath them was a door: the only other one in the room.

Thomas pointed towards a big **X** on the wall to the left. 'This must be the first of the main challenges.'

'O-kay, and about time, too' Finlay said. 'I'll ask the question again: who is going to be jousting who?'

CLANK!

'Oh no,' Thomas said. 'It's the knight!'

'Maybe we should go back,' Finlay said, edging away.

Thomas grabbed him by the arm. 'There's no point in running away. If the knight is coming, we need to face him.'

'But ...' Finlay said, ready to protest.

'No buts. We can do this. We've got this far, so there's no reason we can't get past this. Get through this and we'll be a big step closer to getting out of here.'

CLANK!

Finlay said. 'What if we have to face something far worse than a knight next?'

This got Thomas wondering: what if there *was* something far worse? He tried to not show how worried he was, because he knew this would make Finlay even more anxious.

'Let's not worry about that for now,' Thomas said. 'One problem at a time, yeah?'

Finlay gave a weak nod. 'One problem at a time,' he repeated.

'Those lances look heavy,' Thomas noted. 'I don't know how I'll be able to hold one of those up.' He was relieved to see that both of them had rounded balls at the striking ends. 'The riddle mentioned the lances, which I see. It mentioned horses, which I can see. I'm guessing the tilt is the plastic barrier. But where are the two suits of armour?'

'And the squire?'

CLANK! CLANK! CLANK!

The door beneath the digital displays opened and a knight entered the room. Light glinted off his plastic armour as he made his way across the room towards the horse at the far end. Tomas noted, with some alarm, that he had a sword sheathed at his side. Then the knight mounted his horse, picked up the lance that was resting against it and looked towards the boys.

'I'm n-not facing you without any a-a-armour,' Thomas stammered.

The knight gestured with his lance and Thomas saw that a pile of plastic armour had appeared at the end of the tilt, next to the horse that would be his ride.

'I know who the squire is meant to be,' Finlay said. 'It's me. I'm supposed to help dress you up in that lot.'

Thomas had never seen Finlay look so afraid. He wanted to pull him close, hug him, tell him everything would be okay, but he knew his brother wouldn't believe any reassurances he could give him.

'We *can* do this,' Thomas said, kneeling in front of Finlay and looking him intently in the eyes. Thomas mulled over how he could inspire him to be brave. And then it came to Thomas ... 'Hey, can you remember when that boy was bullying you at school and you were too afraid to go?'

Finlay nodded. 'Karl Gates: the biggest boy in my year. He used to give me dead arms and Chinese burns.'

'Yes, he used to – he doesn't anymore. Because we stood up to him.'

'*You* stood up to him.'

'No,' Thomas said, '*we* stood up to him. We approached him in the playground, when his friends weren't around to back him up. I asked him to stop picking on you and he told me to get lost, remember?'

'I thought he was going to punch you.'

'So did I. But I was determined not to show him how scared I was, so I stood my ground – *we* stood our ground. I knew that he had to be the one to walk away from us if we wanted to put an end to the bullying. And he did, eventually, when he realised that his threats weren't working. Oh man, I think he must have called us every name under the sun.'

'He called you a booger-snot,' Finlay said, managing a half-smile.

'And he called you a melon-head, if I remember right,' Thomas said.

'I still don't know what a melon-head is.'

'Neither does he, most likely. And he's probably too dumb to be able to spell it. I know he's given you the dead-eye since then, but that's all he's done; he hasn't bothered you like he used to.'

'No, he hasn't,' Finlay agreed. 'But why are you reminding me about that now?'

Clank! Clank! Clank! The knight banged his fist on his leg, then pointed towards the other horse.

'I'm reminding you about it,' Thomas said to Finlay, 'because that knight over there is just another bully. We dealt with Karl Gates by sticking together and being brave and that's what we're going to do now – we're going to stick together and deal with this rusty bucket of ... plastic. Are you with me?'

'Yes,' Finlay said, not looking confident.

'Imagine that's Karl Gates over there in that armour,' Thomas said. 'You can't tell me that you wouldn't love to knock him off a horse and send him sprawling.'

Finlay's eyes narrowed and a spark of determination fired inside him. 'Now that would be *awesome!*'

CLANK! CLANK! CLANK! The knight banged on his leg again, then jabbed his finger towards the horse.

'Let's go and get him,' Finlay said, leading the way.

Thomas felt proud of his brother as he followed behind him. *Not sure I'd have been so brave at his age*, he thought. Thomas was now shaking because he was so terrified, but he was adamant not to show any sign of this, if he could help it.

Putting the armour on proved to be a slow and laborious affair. It took them a few minutes just to fit the breastplate and the rest of the suit wasn't any easier to don. By the time they were half-done, the knight was really beginning to get impatient.

CLANK! CLANK! CLANK! CLANK!

'Sorry to keep you waiting, but we're doing this as fast as we can,' Thomas said. 'It's weird how his plastic armour makes that sound, as if it's made of metal.'

'I hope he stays sat on that horse,' Finlay said, snatching nervous glances in the knight's direction. 'What if he decides to come over here? What if he decides that he doesn't want to joust us and that he wants to use his sword instead?'

Thomas wondered what sort of damage could be inflicted with a plastic sword. A fatal, slicing blow, or a stinging whack? He hoped he would not find out the answer to this question.

He said, 'Number one: keep your voice down or you might put ideas into his head. Number two: just concentrate on getting this armour on me. And number three: we don't have swords to fight him with and I'm pretty sure it's a fair fight he's looking for.'

'If a suit of armour can appear out of nothing, then so can some swords. Why would you assume he wants a fair fight? How can you possibly know that?'

'I was taught that knights were supposed to be chivalrous.'

'What does that mean?'

'It means to be brave, courteous and honourable.'

'It's not hard to be brave when you're up against a seven year old and a ten year old. And who's to say that this knight is courteous and honourable.'

'I'd say the fact that he hasn't already charged at us is a good indicator, given how long it's taking you to dress me in this getup.'

CLANK! CLANK! CLANK! CLANK! CLANK!

'All right, all right,' Thomas said, 'we're nearly done.'

Finlay fitted the gauntlets over Thomas's wrists, and then Thomas donned the helmet.

'Okay,' Finlay said, stepping back so he could look him up and down, 'I think you're ready.'

'I could never be ready for this,' Thomas said. 'Wish me luck.' *I think I'm going to need it*, he thought.

'What do you suppose will happen if you lose?' Finlay said.

'I knew you were going to ask me that.' Thomas shrugged. *Maybe he'll show us how good he is with that sword*, he thought, but he didn't say this. 'Losing is not an option.' Thomas went to mount his horse, but he couldn't quite manage it. 'This armour is hard to move in; I don't think I'll be able to get on without some help.'

Finlay gave him a boost up, and then that was it: Thomas was on his horse and nearly ready. Mustering all his strength, he picked up the lance and pointed it out in front of him.

'I can hardly hold this thing up,' he said, his muscles already straining. 'It's a lot heavier than I thought it would be.' He let the front end drop and then looked towards the knight. 'How can I joust you if I can't even hold my lance up?'

The only response the knight gave was to raise his own lance to indicate he was ready.

'Do you even know how to speak?' Thomas asked him. 'I'm not strong enough to hold up my lance, *so HOW can I joust you?*'

The knight didn't respond, didn't move a muscle; he just continued to hold his long spear out to show he was ready.

BLEEP!

The top digital display began to count down from 10 ...

'Oh great,' Thomas said. 'I'm done for.' He focused his attention once again on the knight. 'It's not very chivalrous to mow down someone who can't defend themselves, you know.'

... 6 ... 5 ... 4 ...

'How brave and bold of you,' Finlay chimed in. 'You're about to beat a kid who can't even defend himself.'

'This could be the most one-sided jousting contest

ever in the history of jousting contests,' Thomas
commented.

... 3 ... 2 ... 1 ...

'No it won't be,' Finlay said. He climbed onto the
back of the horse and positioning himself behind his
brother.

'What are you doing?' Thomas said.

'Helping you,' Finlay replied. 'You can't hold the
lance up on your own, but maybe both of us can.'

'But you're not wearing any armour.'

'I'm behind you, so I don't need any armour.'

Thomas went to open his mouth to tell his brother,
no way, you're not taking part in this, but Thomas
knew there was no other option.

He dropped the visor on his helmet.

Then a whirring sound filled the room as the
mechanism that drove the horses stirred to life.

'Okay, but you make sure you keep your head out
of harm's way,' Thomas said as they picked up the
lance together and held it out in front of them. 'No
peaking around me to see what's happening,
otherwise you could get your head taken off, yeah.'

Finlay assured him that he wouldn't. 'Crikey, you
were right – this thing weighs a tonne. We're going to
struggle even with two of us holding it.'

A buzzer sounded and both horses began moving
towards each other: slowly, at first – and then they
picked up speed.

'Aim for the centre of his chest,' Finlay advised.

I'll try, Thomas thought, bracing himself for the worst. He raised the lance, lining it up as best as he could, and then ...

BOOM!

... it was Thomas who took a hit to the chest. The force of the blow knocked the breath out of him and sent him tumbling backwards. Somehow, he managed to avoid crushing Finlay as they both crashed to the padded floor.

'Ouch,' Thomas said, struggling to breathe for a few seconds. 'That hurt ... as much as ... I thought it would.'

Flat on his back, Finlay looked over at his brother and said, 'That's it, we've lost. We're done for now!'

'Are you hurt?'

'No, not hurt,' Finlay said, sitting up. 'Just worried about what's going to happen next.'

'Help me up,' Thomas said.

Finlay lifted him to a sitting position.

Then a bleep sounded a change to the bottom display, which now read: 1 – 0.

'It must be the best of three or something,' Thomas said.

'So we're still in with a chance?'

'Looks that way.'

After the boys had been unseated, both horses had kept moving along the track. Reaching the end, they'd turned around so they were once again facing each other.

BLEEP!

The top display began counting down from 10 again ...

Thomas held out a hand to Finlay, who grasped it and yanked him to his feet. Thomas picked up his lance.

Making their way back towards their horse, the boys discussed tactics.

'Perhaps we should aim at his head this time,' Finlay suggested.

'That's a much smaller target. We could easily miss.'

'We could. But if we *don't* miss, we're going to clean his clock.'

As they walked, Thomas gave this some thought.

'Or,' Finlay added, 'we could just try and aim for his chest again and hope for the best.' He waited for a reply. When one wasn't forthcoming, he said, 'Are you even listening to me? Earth to Thomas! Hullo – Earth to Thomas!

'I'm still thinking! Don't go on at me; I *hate* it went you do that. It fries my brain, it really does.'

'There's no more time for thinking,' Finlay said, nodding towards the top display, which was now showing a big, fat zero.

'We'll try for the head,' Thomas said, going with Finlay's suggestion.

Finlay helped him back on their horse, then seated himself behind him.

'If it's the best of three and we lose this,' Thomas said, 'we're done for.'

'Best not lose then.'

Easier said than done, Thomas thought.

Then the buzzer sounded and the plastic horses once again began to advance towards each other. Like last time: slowly, at first – and then they picked up speed.

The knight raised his lance. Thomas and Finlay raised theirs and ...

BOOM!

... they caught the knight in the face with a glancing blow, which skimmed off the side of his helmet. Unfortunately, at the same time, the rounded end of the knight's lance hit Thomas squarely in the chest. Then, just like last time, the boys fell backwards. But, unlike last time, Thomas landed on top of Finlay, crushing Finlay's leg.

'*Owww-WWW!*' he yelled, crying out in pain as he tried to push his brother off. 'Get off me! Get ... *off MEEE!*'

With a great deal of effort, Thomas managed to roll himself to one side, away from Finlay.

Removing his helmet, Thomas tossed it aside. 'Are you okay?' he asked Finlay. 'You haven't broken anything, have you?'

'I don't know,' Finlay replied, grimacing whilst clutching his leg. 'I don't think so.'

'If you'd broken something, I think you'd know

about it by now.'

Thomas knelt by him, then glanced towards the bottom display, which now read: 2-0.

The knight got off his horse and advanced towards them.

'Erm,' Thomas said, 'I know you're in pain and all that, but now might be a good time to get up and start moving, because plastic head is coming our way.'

'Oh poo,' Finlay said, following his gaze. Seeming to forget about the pain, Finlay sprang to his feet and helped Thomas up. 'Going for the head wasn't such a good idea after all.'

'Forget about that,' Thomas said. He nodded towards the knight, who was closing the gap between them at a surprisingly quick speed. 'What are we going to do about *him*?'

Any second now he was sure that the knight would draw his sword and either slash or bash them with it. So Thomas thought it might be a good idea to start begging.

'Please don't hurt us,' he said, backing away with Finlay at his side. 'If you give us another chance at jousting you, I'm sure we can do better. We could do the best of five, yeah? What do you say?'

The knight said nothing. He continued to advance and the boys continued to back away, heading towards the door beneath the displays.

'I'm sorry I moaned that I was bored,' Thomas said. 'I shouldn't have done it and I'm REALLY sorry. Just don't chop us into bits, okay! *PLEASE* don't hurt us!'

Finlay lost his footing and fell backwards, dragging Thomas down with him. With the knight almost upon them, Thomas embraced his brother, hugging him tight. Thomas noticed that Finlay had closed his eyes and so he followed suit. *It's going to happen any second now*, Thomas thought. *He's going to unsheathe that sword and ...*

Click! ... BANG!

Thomas opened his eyes and looked around.

The knight had disappeared.

Thomas assumed that the clicking sound must have been the door's lock disengaging and that the BANG had been the door shutting.

'He's gone,' he said. 'We're okay, he's gone.' Never in his life could he remember feeling so relieved. 'Woo-hoo! He's gone!' Finlay's eyes were still firmly clamped shut, so Thomas gave him a shake. 'We're all right, plastic head has disappeared!'

Finlay opened one of his eyes and then the other. 'Where'd he go?'

'Through the door, I think.'

'Why didn't he attack us?'

Thomas shook his head. 'I have no idea. But I don't want to hang around here, just in case he changes his mind. Help me out of this armour, squire.'

As the boys stood up, Finlay clutched at his leg and grimaced.

'That bad, huh?' Thomas said.

'Yes,' Finlay replied, 'That bad.'

'You might just have a dead leg. Pull your bottoms down so I can take a look.'

Finlay did as his brother advised.

'There's no red mark or anything,' Thomas said, 'so it can't be too bad. Be thankful that it isn't a breakage. Try and walk a bit.'

'You're not a doctor, so how can you know whether it's broken or not?'

'You're right, I'm not a doctor. But you've just stood up, haven't you? I'd say that was a pretty good indicator. Now do as I suggested: try and walk around a bit.'

Finlay winced as he took a few tentative steps.

'Go on,' Thomas said, encouraging him. 'Keep going; you're doing well.'

After taking six or seven more steps, Finlay turned to his brother and said, 'It doesn't seem quite so bad now that I'm moving about. 'The pins and needles are going, so that's a good sign, isn't it?'

'It is,' Thomas confirmed. 'Must be a dead leg, just like I said.'

Finlay hobbled back to Thomas, then helped him out of the armour.

'I'm glad to be out of that get-up,' Thomas commented. 'I was sweating cobs underneath that lot.'

Finlay tried the door that the knight had disappeared through.

'Locked?' Thomas said.

Finlay gave a disappointed nod. 'So we've lost the first big challenge. Does that mean that we have to win the next two?'

'The next two main ones, yes. It's looking that way.'

'Grrr-eat.'

'The next time you give me advice about what to do in any situation, I'm going to ignore you.'

'I didn't twist your arm behind your back and force you to aim at his head. I just suggested it because trying to hit him in the chest hadn't worked ...'

Holding up a finger, Thomas motioned Finlay to be quiet.

'What's wrong?' Finlay said.

'*Shhh!* Keep your trap shut, will you. Can't you hear it?'

'Hear what?' Finlay said. And then he did hear it: voices. This sent his imagination into overdrive. 'I bet it's the knight coming back with some other knights. They're coming to dish out our punishment for losing.'

Thomas could see from the look on Finlay's face that they were both thinking the same thing: what could that punishment be? Nothing life-threatening, he figured – otherwise they wouldn't be able to continue with the challenges.

'Maybe we should hide?' Finlay suggested.

'Hide where? There's nothing to hide behind.'

'We need to do *something*. We can't just stand here

and wait and hope for the best!'

The voices grew louder as whoever was coming got closer.

'It's coming from behind that door,' Thomas said, gesturing towards the one beneath the digital displays.

Finlay hobbled towards the lance and went to pick it up.

'What are you doing?' Thomas asked him.

'We can use this to fend them off. Come on, help me; I can't lug this thing on my own.'

Thomas helped Finlay pick up the lance and they readied themselves with it.

The voices were very close now: literally on the other side of the door. Thomas and Finlay could hear what was being said:

'Do you think we'll find the other two?'

'I dunno. Maybe.'

'They might have made it out. Perhaps they've made it out and told our parents where we are, which would mean help is on the way.'

'You can believe that, if it makes you feel better.'

'Should we go through this door or the other one?'

'I've got a good feeling about this one, but I'm up for an eenie meenie miney mo if you are?'

Finlay and Thomas looked at each other excitedly.

Thomas said, 'That's Brady ...'

'... and Ella,' Finlay said, finishing his sentence.

Thomas and Finlay dropped the lance. They went

towards the door: Thomas running and Finlay hobbling behind him. Just before Thomas reached the door, it creaked open a bit and Brady stuck his head through the gap, checking things out before he entered.

'It *is* you,' Thomas said, greeting him with a warm smile. 'I knew I recognised the voices.'

Brady was just as happy to see Thomas as Thomas was to see him.

'Why are you limping?' Ella said to Finlay as she entered the room with her brother. 'Have you hurt yourself?'

Thomas told them about everything that'd happened. He explained about how he and Finlay had built the makeshift stairs using soft play blocks, so they could exit the courtyard before the knight entered. He explained about the Nerf arrows that'd bombarded them as they'd crossed the balance beam and how something had stirred beneath the plastic balls, giving them the heebie jeebies. And, finally, Thomas gave a very detailed account of the jousting contest that'd just taken place and how they had lost two nil in a best of three.

'So where's the knight now?' Brady said.

Finlay nodded towards the door that Brady and Ella had just entered through. 'After we lost, he disappeared through there. Or at least that's where we think he went. Did you see him? If not, you must have missed him by seconds.'

'We didn't notice any knight,' Ella said.

'You "think" he went through the door?' Brady said to Thomas. 'Didn't you see him leave?'

'No,' he replied. 'When we lost the second time, I landed on Finlay so I was too busy dealing with the fact that I might have broken his leg to notice if the knight had vanished.'

Finlay shot Thomas a look, communicating a clear message: why are you lying?

Because, Thomas thought, *I don't want to tell them we were cowering like cowards, with our eyes shut.*

Brady walked towards one of the lances and picked it up. 'Whoa!' he said, struggling to raise it, 'this thing is heavy – how did you battle with it?'

'I rode behind Thomas and helped him out,' Finlay said.

'I've always wondered what it would be like to joust,' Brady said, 'and you pair actually got to do it.' He noticed the pile of armour by the tilt. 'Whoa! Did you wear that lot?'

'I did,' Thomas confirmed. 'For all the good it did us.'

'Well, it is all made from plastic,' Brady noted.

'No, that wasn't the problem,' Thomas said. 'The knight was just too good for us.'

'How did you pair get in?' Finlay asked Brady and Ella. He focused his attention on Ella, who was twirling her hair with her fingers. 'You were adamant that you wouldn't come in here, because you were so scared. What changed your mind?'

It was Brady who answered the question: 'After you left and the drawbridge was raised, she got even more scared when it was just the two of us. We banged on that door for about ten minutes and then gave up. As I was walking away, I noticed that a door had appeared in the wall at the far end of the room, so we went to investigate.'

Luka remembered the wall and recalled how he'd wondered what was behind it.

Brady enlightened him: 'There was a riddle on the door. It took us a while to solve, but we got there in the end. We were hopeful that we'd found a way out, but I should have known it wouldn't be that simple. When we *did* find out what was behind it, Ella had a complete meltdown again. She burst into tears, blubbering about how there was no way she was going to go into a maze ...'

'I did not blubber!' Ella protested.

'Yes you did,' Brady said.

'Did not!' Ella hissed.

'I've always enjoyed working my way through mazes,' Finlay said.

'You wouldn't have enjoyed this one,' Brady said. 'It took me a while to make Ella realise that going into the maze was the only option, but I got through to her in the end. Every route we took through it, we hit a dead end or ended up coming back on ourselves. The problem was that it all looked the same, so we couldn't tell where we'd been and where we hadn't. And we were sure we heard someone laughing at one point, which really scared the heck out of Ella.'

Ella chirped in: 'You were scared, too. And don't try and act like you weren't.'

'I never said that I wasn't, did I?' Brady said. He continued with his story. 'It took us ages to find our way through, but we eventually got out. After we came out of the maze, we entered a corridor, which took us to two doors. We obviously chose the right one.'

'You told us you had to solve a riddle,' Finlay said to him. 'What was it about?'

'I can't remember how it went exactly, but it mentioned things like broomsticks, a wand, books of spells, a pointy hat ...'

'Was the answer a witch?' Finlay speculated.

'No,' Ella said, 'that was our first guess. The answer was a wizard.'

Something occurred to Thomas: 'So far, all the riddles we've solved have given us clues about things that are going to happen. I hope this doesn't mean that we've got to face a wizard. The knight was bad enough.'

'I don't know any magic,' Ella said.

'Neither do any of us,' Thomas put in.

'You told us that you lost twice to the knight,' Brady said, 'and yet nothing happened to you. He just strolled past you and left the room. Why do you think that was?'

Thomas said, 'Because jousting was only the first of three main challenges.'

Producing the note from his pocket, he unfolded it and handed it to Brady.

'We found that in the courtyard,' Thomas said. 'Pinned to a wall.'

Brady read through it with widening eyes. Ella joined him at his side and read it as well.

'J.T.?' Brady said. 'Who's J.T.?'

'We think it's the old guy who owns the play centre,' Finlay said. 'Did he tell you his name when he booked you and Ella in?'

'No,' Ella said. 'Not that I can remember.'

Brady shook his head to confirm this.

He pointed to the **X** on the wall. 'You've done other challenges,' he said. 'You built a staircase from blocks and you had to go over that beam while being pelted with Nerf arrows ...'

'We saw no Xs when we did those,' Finlay said. 'The note clearly states that the main challenges are marked with an X.'

Finlay scanned the note again. 'The last bit worries me. It doesn't sound good. What do you think it means by "Lose on the other hand and things could get heated. You'll disappear in the blink of an eye as if you've been deleted."?'

'No idea,' Thomas said. 'But you're right; it doesn't sound good.'

'Facing a wizard could be the next big challenge,' Brady said, 'the second in the best of three. If that's the case, we mustn't lose – otherwise it could mean ...' He ran a finger across his throat to convey what he was thinking, and immediately regretted it when he saw the look on Ella's face. 'But we won't lose,' he assured her. 'There's four of us now, so we've got double the chance of winning.'

'I think you could be right,' Thomas said, 'but I hope you're wrong. If we couldn't beat a knight, what chance have we got against a wizard?'

'If we face him thinking we're going to be defeated, then we'll be defeated,' Brady said. 'The only way we can win is if we *believe* we can.'

'He talks sense,' Finlay said.

'Okay,' Thomas said. 'So which door do we go through now? My guess is that it's the one the knight just went through.'

They tried it – but it was locked.

'What about the one on the far side?' Ella said, pointing.

'It's probably locked,' Thomas explained. 'And you wouldn't want to go that way anyway. It wouldn't be any easier. That's how we got here: through there.'

'Yeah, just trust us on this one,' Finlay said. 'You really don't want to go back that way.'

'Looks like it'll have to be that one, then,' Ella said, gesturing towards a door at the far end.

'That wasn't there before,' Finlay noted.

A door popping into existence out of nowhere did not come as a surprise to Thomas. Weird and whacky things were happening all around him and he only expected more of same as things progressed.

As they all made their way across the room, Brady asked Thomas if the knight had been armed with a sword.

'He was,' Thomas said. 'A plastic one. Sheaved at his side.'

'Plastic?' Brady said. 'What good would a plastic sword be? Other than whacking somebody, what damage would you be able to do with it?'

'Fortunately, we never found out,' Thomas said. 'And in this place, who knows? Plastic might cut like metal. It sounds daft, I know. But given everything that's happened so far ...'

'Nothing would surprise you,' Brady said, finishing his sentence. 'Nothing would surprise me, either.'

Reaching the door, Thomas checked to see if it was unlocked. It was, so he asked everyone if they were ready. Blank expressions suggested they weren't, but he opened the door anyway.

'More fun and games,' Thomas said, looking along the corridor ahead of them, which was filled with punch bags. 'O-kay, so what do we have to do here?'

The others followed him through the doorway and Ella let out a high-pitched yelp as the door clicked shut behind them.

'Did you have to do that?' Finlay said. 'You scared me.'

Ella shot him a reproachful glare. 'Sorry,' she hissed. 'I'm just a little bit on edge, if that's all right.'

Finlay took a step away from her, and then another – just to be on the safe side.

'I don't see an X anywhere,' he said.

'Not one of the big three challenges, then,' Brady noted. 'I think we're supposed to put these on,' he said, picking up a bag full of boxing gloves. 'There's two big pairs and two small pairs.' He handed them to the others and they began slipping them on, fastening the Velcro straps.

'Well this should be easy enough,' Brady said. 'And quite fun. I always enjoy whacking these things out of the way.'

'I don't think this is going to be as easy as it looks,' Thomas said. 'Nothing else has been so far and I can't see this being any different.'

Sure enough, something began to happen. The bags started to stretch and expand, like something was trying to burst out ...

'What's happening?' Ella said, backing away.

Noticing that she still hadn't put on one of her gloves, Thomas slid it over her hand and secured the strap.

'Don't worry,' he said to her. 'We'll deal with whatever is coming – you just follow behind us.'

Ella gave a weak nod and Thomas turned his

attention to the bags, which had now sprouted arms ... with boxing gloves on the hands.

'Oh ... *what!*' Thomas said, shaking his head. 'This keeps getting weirder and weirder.'

'Punch bags that fight back,' Finlay said. 'Grrrr-eat.'

'So who's going first?' Brady said. When everyone looked at him, he added, 'Looks like it's me, then.'

'You are the biggest,' Ella pointed out.

'I've watched boxing on telly,' Thomas said. We need to keep our hands up to protect ourselves and our chins down, so we don't get knocked out.'

'Will they hit us that hard?' Finlay said.

'Not if we float like a butterfly and sting like a bee,' Brady said, shuffling his feet back and forth.

'How's that leg now?' Thomas asked Finlay. 'Are you good to go for this?'

Finlay gave his leg a shake and replied: 'It's okay now. Nearly back to one hundred percent.'

'Good stuff,' Thomas said. He gestured Brady to lead the way. 'Show us how this floating like a butterfly and stinging like a bee should be done.'

Psyching himself up, Brady turned his rage towards the punch bags, then charged forwards, bashing the first one out of the way with a straight right. As he went to advance, however, he got caught with a left hook to the side of the head and went down to his knees. Before any of the others could move to help him, he got back to his feet and kept moving as he gave out blows and received some.

'Right,' Thomas said to the other two, 'I'm going to be moving fast to try and smash a way through for you, so make sure you stay with me, yeah?'

Finlay and Ella assured him they would.

Setting off at a rapid pace, Thomas smashed his way past one punch bag, and then another, and then another. As he turned to see if the others were following, he got hit with a glancing blow, which was just enough to disorientate him for a second. Another blow caught him in the gut, knocking the wind out of him. He was about to go down when Finlay and Ella caught up with him. Taking an arm each, they kept him moving whilst bashing bags out the way with their spare hands.

Up ahead, Brady had stopped and was swinging wildly in all directions. 'Come on, you three!' he rasped. 'Get a move on!'

Thomas wondered how long the corridor might be and how many bags they would have to smash before they reached the other end. 'I'm okay,' he said, shrugging Finlay and Ella off, then charging ahead. 'Keep punching!'

They kept moving forwards, dishing out blows and taking them.

'*Woo-hoo!*' Ella exclaimed, bashing and smashing.

'*Woo-hoo!*' Finlay yelled, following suit.

As Thomas ploughed forwards, he came upon Brady, who was sprawled on the floor, looking dazed.

Noticing that there weren't many bags left in front of them, Thomas grabbed him by the wrist and began dragging him. For a second he forgot about Finlay and Ella. He concentrated on nothing but getting Brady to safety. When Thomas had dragged Brady clear of danger, he turned his attention to the others.

'*Ow!*' he heard Finlay say. 'That hurt!'

'Just keep moving!' he heard Ella say.

They emerged: Finlay first, and then Ella.

'Yay!' Ella said, punching out at thin air. 'We made it through! That was fun – I enjoyed it.' She noticed her brother on the floor and forgot all about beating up punch bags. 'Are you okay?' she asked him, concerned. 'You look like a drunkard who's collapsed.'

'I'm punch drunk,' Brady replied, clutching at his guts. 'I'll be all right in a minute, when I get my breath back.'

'Are you okay?' Thomas asked Finlay.

'Yeah,' he said, smiling a toothy smile. 'That was the most fun I've had in a long time.'

'*Fun!*' Brady said, still clutching his guts. 'Is being *punched* your idea of fun?'

'You don't get punched when you move like a butterfly and sting like a bee,' Ella said, shuffling her feet back and forth.

She removed her gloves and let them drop to the floor. Everyone else removed theirs.

'Ha-ha, very funny,' Brady said. 'If you don't make

it as a boxer when you're older, you can always try out as a comedian. Go on, have another run through if you want. But you might not be so lucky this time – you might get clobbered a good 'un.'

'There was no luck involved,' Ella said reproachfully. 'I was just good at dodging the punches.'

'Go on, then,' Brady said, repeating himself, 'have another run through. We'll wait here for you, sis.'

She looked towards the punch bags, and then towards the gloves by her feet, as if she was considering Brady's suggestion. The gloved hands of the bags were hanging limply by their sides, but Thomas knew that they would spring back to life and start swinging if anyone came within range.

'You've proven you're brave,' Thomas said to Ella, 'you don't need to do it again.' He turned his attention to Brady, who was still on the floor. 'Are you okay to get up now,' Thomas asked him, offering him a hand.

Taking the hand, Brady allowed himself to be yanked to his feet.

'Your sister is quite a Jekyll and Hyde character,' Thomas whispered to him. 'One minute she's in tears and begging to be let out, and the next she thinks she can take on Mike Tyson.'

'Yep, that's my sister in a nutshell,' Brady replied.

'I'm sorry, what was that?' Ella said, advancing towards them. 'Are you pair talking about me?'

'No,' Thomas and Brady said in unison. They both

did a poor impression of not looking guilty as charged.

'What next, I wonder,' Brady said, changing the subject. 'As long as it's not something that involves me being hit, then I'll be happy.'

'I'm not so sure you will,' Thomas said, focusing on what lay ahead of them. At the end of the corridor was yet another door (Thomas was getting sick of seeing doors). He wondered what on earth could be behind this one. A voice spoke up in his head: *the wizard, of course – it's going to be the wizard.*

'Please don't let there be another riddle,' Finlay said. 'I don't think I can bear another one.'

Thankfully, the door was mercifully free of riddles.

'I'm sure we've already solved the riddle for what's coming next,' Thomas said, opening the door.

As everyone stepped inside the next area, Brady let out a troubled moan. 'No, no, *no*,' he said. 'Not *this* again. We've already been through the maze once, so why do we have to do it again?'

Ahead of them was a passage that terminated with the option of going either left or right.

'Okay, okay,' Thomas said, 'let's not panic. The fact that you've already been through can only be a good thing, yeah? You made it out last time, so I'm sure we can do it this time. Nothing tried to eat you while you were in there, did it?'

'No,' Brady said.

'And nothing attacked you?'

'No,' Brady admitted.

'Nothing jumped out and scared you?'

'No,' Ella said. 'But we're sure we heard someone laughing at us and that *did* scare us.'

'We've got this far by working together,' Thomas said. 'Me and Finlay worked as a team to build the stairs using blocks and we battled the knight together. You pair worked together to get through the maze the first time. And that's how we're going to get through this and beat this wizard: by sticking *together* and working as a *team*. Plus, the maze may take us back to where we started – back to the first door we came through that got us into all this trouble.'

'Back to square one, you mean,' Finlay said.

Thomas shrugged. 'Maybe that's what's supposed to happen. Maybe we're supposed to end up back where we started. The door might open now.'

'And it might not,' Ella said. 'We haven't done all three big challenges yet, so surely we wouldn't be able to get out even if we did end up back at square one. *And* we might not get back to that door. Who's to say that we won't just go round in a big circle and wind up back here. Or we could leave the maze through another exit and be even more lost than ever.'

'We're on the right track,' Thomas said, gesturing towards a big X on the wall, 'and that's all we need to know. We'll end up wherever we end up.'

'He is right,' Brady said, seeing the logic of what Thomas was saying. 'The answer to the riddle was a wizard, and we're going to find him in this maze. We just need to accept that and move forwards. It's the only way.'

'Come on, we showed those punch bags who was boss,' Thomas said, trying to spur everyone on, 'now let's show the wizard!'

'Brady didn't show the punch bags who was boss,' Ella said. 'He ended up on the floor.'

Brady gave her a sharp look. 'You're going to be on the floor in a minute if you don't shut up!'

'Please, you pair,' Thomas said, appealing for calm, 'let's just concentrate on what's happening next. Brady, you should lead the way.'

'Why me?'

'Because you made it through last time,' Thomas said. 'You must be able to remember something about the layout, yeah?'

'It's a maze,' Brady said, 'I can't remember anything about how I got through it.'

'Neither can I,' Ella admitted.

'We just kept going until we got out,' Brady said.

'I still think you should lead the way,' Thomas said.

'Fine,' Brady said. 'For all the good it'll do us. I've got a bad feeling that it's going to be more difficult this time.'

'I've got a bad feeling it is, too,' Ella said.

'Can we stop the talking and just get moving?' Finlay said.

'Fine,' Brady said again. 'Just make sure we all stay

together. If we lose someone in here, it's going to make things doubly difficult.'

CHAPTER
FOUR

(the Wizard and the Maze)

'This isn't the way we entered last time,' Brady said, setting off, 'so I don't suppose it matters whether we go left or right.'

Reaching the end of the passage, he veered left with no hesitation. The others followed.

They went down another passage – took a right, then a left, then another right – and came face-to-face with a dead end.

'There's lots of those in here,' Brady said.

They backtracked and took another route. As they walked, Thomas looked up at the padded walls, wondering if he'd be able to see over them if Brady gave him a leg-up.

'It's too high,' Brady said. 'I already tried it with Ella.'

'But I'm taller than her,' Thomas said.

'Not tall enough,' Brady said.

His voice echoed into the air, indicating the vastness of the area they were now in.

They continued walking: exploring passages, meeting dead-ends and doubling back on themselves ...

'Our parents must be going out of their brains with worry by now,' Finlay said.

'For all the good it'll do us,' Brady said.

'My mum isn't someone to be messed with, though,' Finlay said. 'She'll be giving that guy behind the counter absolute hell about this. She'll be insisting that he call the police and all sorts.'

'Again,' Brady said, 'for all the good it'll do us.'

After a few seconds of silence, mulling things over, Finlay added: 'If only you'd kept your gob shut,

Thomas. If only you hadn't been such a grouch-face booger-snot.'

'What does he mean?' Ella asked. 'If only he'd kept his gob shut about what?'

'*Thanks*,' Thomas said to Finlay, giving him an icy stare. 'Thanks for mentioning that, little brother.'

Ella looked puzzled. 'What's being a grouch-face booger-snot got to do with us being in here?'

Thomas didn't reply.

When Ella asked the same question again, Finlay said, 'We may as well just tell them. I think they have the right to know why this is happening to them, Thomas.'

Brady stopped dead in his tracks, bringing everyone to a halt. 'The right to know what?' he said, giving Thomas a curious sideways glance. 'You may as well just tell us, because we're not moving until you do.'

'Okay,' Thomas said. 'But just so you know, there was no way I could have known that this would happen. *And* we don't know for sure that it is my whinging that's caused us to be here.'

'Whinging?' Brady said. 'What are you talking about?'

It was Finlay who gave the explanation: 'Before we came here, to the play centre, Thomas had moaned about having to come off his XBOX. He told our parents that he didn't want to go because he said it would be boring. In the car, all the way here he moaned about how boring it was going to be. And when we got here and met the man behind the counter, he moaned some more. So we think it was all that moaning – that *whinging!* – about how bored he was that's caused this to happen. We think that the old man is trying to make things more exciting for us.'

'More exciting? More ex … citing,' Ella said slowly, as if tasting every syllable of the words. 'Well, he's certainly done that.' She shouted up into the air: '*And terrifying, too!*' Her voice echoed throughout the cavernous space, bouncing here and there with surprising clarity.

'We're just guessing that this is the case,' Thomas said, sporting his best apologetic look. He'd expected Brady to be angry, but he didn't seem angry at all. Not in the slightest.

'*You* were moaning when you came in as well,' Ella said, turning her fury towards her brother. 'Whining about why we had to go to the play centre instead of somewhere better. When the old man asked you why you looked so miserable, you told him that you'd rather go bowling.'

Brady was now also sporting an apologetic look. 'Hey, don't blame me,' he protested. 'Let's not jump to conclusions here. As Thomas pointed out, we can't know for sure that one or two of us whinging about being bored is what's caused this. Although I must admit, it is an explanation that fits. But then I'd say it's a bit extreme to inflict all this on us just 'cause we were a bit grouchy. There could be more to this than meets the eye – don't you think?'

'There could be,' Ella said. 'Or it really *could* be you that's to blame.'

'Look,' Thomas said, appealing for calm, 'there's no point in trying to point the finger of blame here. That really isn't going to help. Although if you *do* want to blame anyone, I'd say the old guy behind the counter should be the one (assuming he's responsible, of course).'

'Oh he's going to get an earful from me when we get out of here, don't you worry about that,' Ella said. 'I'll box his ears off, like I did with those punch bags.'

I wouldn't want to be him if we do make it out of here, Thomas thought.

Finlay held up a finger, silencing everyone. 'Did you hear that?'

'Hear what?' Brady asked.

'*Listen!*' Finlay said, still holding up his finger.

And then they all heard it: laughter. Quiet, at first. And then it got louder.

An icy chill ran through Thomas's body.

'That's what we heard last time,' Ella said in a low voice. 'I *knew* we hadn't imagined it.'

'The wizard?' Finlay said. His voice was barely a whisper.

Brady nodded.

A voice boomed throughout the place, making

them all jump: 'It's time to begin!'

'Begin?' Thomas said. 'Begin what?'

All of a sudden, the light began draining out of the room, as if night-time was falling.

Ella shrunk back against the wall, looking afraid.

'It's all right,' Brady said. 'I'm here, so it's all right.' He put an arm around her. 'She's afraid of the dark,' he told the others.

'I'm not too keen on it myself,' Finlay admitted.

The light kept fading, darkness sucking in around them.

'We won't be able to see where we're going,' Ella pointed out. 'How can we get out of the maze if we can't see what we're doing?'

'I'm sure it won't go pitch black,' Brady said. He didn't look hopeful.

Fortunately, it didn't. Ninety percent of the light had faded when the process finally appeared to have come to a halt. Thomas didn't want to open his mouth and jinx the situation. He didn't want to risk making things worse than they were. Finlay, on the other hand, did not have any such reservations.

'Is that it?' he asked. 'Or will it get any darker, do you think?'

Thomas's eyes were beginning to adjust. *I bet that's not the only thing that's going to change,* he thought. 'It's more important than ever that we stick together.'

Coaxing Ella away from the wall, Brady took her hand and said, 'Are you okay to carry on? The sooner we get moving, the sooner we can be out of this place.'

Even though she was scared, she could see that her brother was right. Nodding her head, she gripped his hand tighter.

With his sister in tow, Brady once again led the way, with Thomas taking up the rear.

They reached the end of the passage and went right. Down another passage they all walked. They took a left, a right, another right, and then a left.

'Is any of this looking familiar,' Thomas asked Brady.

'Nope,' came the answer, without any further elaboration.

'Another dead end,' Brady said. He went to double back, but Thomas grabbed him by the arm.

'Hold on a sec,' Thomas said.

He made his way towards the supposed dead end. Putting his hand on one side, he pushed and watched as the end section of the wall opened inwards on a centralised hinge.

Thomas looked back towards the others, whose features were barely discernable now in the darkness. 'Not a dead end, after all,' he said.' It's a panel that pivots.'

As he shouldered his way through one side of the panel, the other side came around behind him, sealing him off from the others. Ahead of him was yet another passage, which was pretty much what

Thomas had expected.

'It's okay, you can come through, you guys,' he said. 'There's nothing to be afraid of.'

When the others didn't follow, he said it again: 'Come on, it's okay – there's nothing to be afraid of.'

When they still didn't follow, Thomas attempted to push his way back through one side of the panel. But it wouldn't budge, so he tried the other side. That wouldn't budge, either.

'Hey, I'm stuck!' Thomas said, beginning to panic. 'If you can just push from your side, we might be able to force it to move. 'Hey, you guys, are you there? Can you hear me?'

There was no reply.

'If this is a joke,' Thomas said, 'I'm not going to be happy. You better not be leaning against the other side of this panel, Finlay.' He doubted this would be the case. He was almost certain the others were too scared to be concerned with pranks, but he preferred to entertain this idea more than the alternative.

Thomas banged his fists on the panel. 'Oh come on, you guys, *please* be there. Tell me you're there! Hello? *Say something!*'

No reply.

'*Heyyyyy!*' Thomas banged his fists some more. '*Hey-YYYYYY!*'

After another minute or so of fist-banging and calling out to the others, he gave up. He stepped back, resigning himself to the alternative that he'd been so keen to dismiss.

'How could I have been so stupid,' he said, cursing himself. 'I can't believe I fell for it!'

Laughter echoed throughout the place. Gooseflesh prickled on the back of Thomas's neck as he span around to face the other way.

'You don't scare me,' he said, trying to sound brave but not doing a convincing job of it.

In the darkness ahead, shadowy shapes morphed and twisted on the walls.

Probably just illusions, Thomas thought.

As he began walking, he was sure that someone or something would reach out and grab him. Any second now one of those shadows would become a hand or a claw and ...

Thomas shook his head, banishing these thoughts.

He pressed on, exploring passages, taking lefts and right, rights and lefts – until, eventually, he reached another dead end. Whilst he was pushing against it to see if it was a pivoting panel, he was sure someone called his name. He listened intently for a while, but he didn't hear anything again. And then, just when he'd given up hope and was convincing himself that it'd been his imagination, he heard it once more. Faint and distant, yes; but someone was *definitely* calling his name. It sounded like Finlay.

'*Finlay!*' Thomas yelled, cupping his hands to his mouth. '*Finlay – can you hear me?*'

He heard a reply (more than one voice was calling

93

out now), but he couldn't make out what was being said.

'I'LL FIND YOU!' Thomas yelled. 'I'LL FIND ALL OF YOU!'

Finlay yelled something back and Thomas caught the last few words: '... *find you, too!*'

Thomas tried to place which direction the voice was coming from, but the echo made it impossible. Thomas still felt relieved, though. Not quite so alone now. His brother was out there somewhere with the others and he was going to find them. No wizard or knight or anything else would stop him from doing so.

Doubling back on himself, he explored more passages, whilst occasionally calling out to the others to see if he was anywhere near them. Sometimes they seemed closer and sometimes they seemed farther away, which frustrated Thomas. And then he remembered what his father had told him and Finlay one time, when they'd been on a day outing to the fun fair:

'If ever you're lost, stay where you are. Don't go looking for us, we'll come and find you. It'll be a lot easier for us to locate you if you don't move.'

Thomas wondered if he should apply this advice to the maze. Should he stay put and let the others find him? Or should he carry on searching? Thomas had always trusted his parents' judgement, so he plumped for the first option. Sitting down, he rested his back

94

against the wall. He pulled his knees up to his chest, then wrapped his arms around his legs.

He waited. And he waited. And he waited some more.

Occasionally he heard the voices of the others: sometimes distant and sometimes seemingly closer. He continued to call out to them in the hope that they would be more successful at honing in on his voice than he'd been at homing in on theirs.

For the first time in his life, Thomas found himself wishing he owned a watch. At least then he'd know how long he'd been lost in the maze and how long they'd been trapped in the secret part of the play centre. Closing his eyes, he counted in his head. He started at one hundred with the intention of working his way back to zero. This, he figured, would help take his mind off his current predicament. And it was working, to a certain extent. Until he got to number seventy-four and a noise close by pulled him out of his thoughts.

Opening his eyes, Thomas looked to his right and could just make out a long shadow forming on the far wall at the end.

Springing to his feet, he watched with concern, wondering who was approaching: friend or foe?

'Finlay – is that you?'

No reply.

'Brady? Ella?'

No reply.

The shadow continued to form, but Thomas didn't wait to see who was casting it. He took to his heels. Off down the passage he went, like his pants were on fire. He ran along another passage, took a left, another left, a right, another left. And then came face to face with a dead end.

'Oh, no,' Thomas muttered.

He turned around and watched in horror as the shadow began forming on the wall at the far end, slithering upwards as if it was somehow alive.

This is it, he thought. *I'm done for.*

He looked around frantically for some way to get out of this situation. Thinking quickly, Thomas realised he had two options. Either he could try and rush past whatever or whoever was pursuing him, or he could attempt to scale one of the walls. He didn't fancy the first option, so he tried the latter. Brady had said that it couldn't be done, but Thomas was going to give it a good try. Moving back as far as he could, Thomas took two big loping steps and then jumped up with all his might. He reached out with his fingers, hoping to grab the top of the wall so he could pull himself up. His effort fell well shy of the height that was needed, though. He lined himself up for a second attempt, but there was no time for this.

At the end of the passage, where the shadow had been forming, now stood a tall, hooded figure. The only discernable feature Thomas could make out was a pair of balefully glowing eyes.

'Please don't hurt me,' Thomas begged, backing away. 'I'm sorry I moaned about being bored, I really am. Just ... please don't hurt me.'

The figure began to advance forwards. It moved soundlessly, as though it was floating. And then, as it raised its arm, Thomas saw that it was holding a long stick, which he presumed was a wand. *It is the wizard!* Thomas thought. *It is him and he's going cast a spell at me!*

As Thomas continued to back away, he wondered what spell the wizard would cast. *Is he about to turn me into a toad? Will he make me disappear in a puff of smoke? Or is he going to just kill me?*

Thomas's retreat was halted abruptly as he backed into the wall that formed the dead end. Realising that the only thing left to do was beg some more, he closed his eyes and gave it his best shot:

'If you let me go I'll be a really good boy from now on,' he blubbered, erupting into an erratic ramble. 'I'll do whatever my parents tell me, *and* I'll keep my room tidy. I'll do all my homework and I won't muck around at school. I won't pick on my little brother *EVER AGAIN!* And ... I'll share all my toys with him and even let him play on my XBOX. Just please ... *PLEASE* don't kill me ... or turn me into a toad ... or make me disappear in a puff of smoke ...'

Suddenly, from behind, Thomas felt the wall fall away from him. As he tumbled backwards, sprawling to the floor, he realised that the dead end had not been a dead end at all. It was a pivoting panel, which had been pushed from the other side by Finlay and the others.

Flat on his back, Thomas looked up at them, focusing mostly on his brother. 'Oh, boy, am I glad to see you lot.'

Then he remembered the wizard and any sense of relief he was feeling disappeared. Not waiting to be helped up, he sprang to his feet and beckoned the others to follow him, which they did without question.

Along passages they went, bounding through the darkness. They took lefts and rights, rights and lefts, until Thomas was sure they were a safe distance from danger.

Bringing everyone to a halt, he put his hands on his knees and took a few seconds to catch his breath. 'Well that wasn't scary at all,' he said. 'Not in the slightest.'

'You sounded pretty scared to me,' Brady said, arming sweat from his brow.

'I was being sarcastic,' Thomas said. 'And you'd have been scared if you'd seen what I've just seen. You'd have pooped your pants.' He explained about the wizard and how he'd been a millisecond away from being zapped with his wand. 'He wasn't what I expected; he was much scarier.'

'What were you expecting?' Ella asked.

Standing up straight, Thomas shrugged. 'I dunno.

An old guy with long, grey hair ... a beard ... wearing a pointy hat ... long, colourful robes ... that sort of thing.'

'And what *did* he look like?' Finlay asked.

Thomas gave him in an in-depth description, then added, 'It was his eyes that unnerved me the most – his glowing eyes.'

'Did he say anything?' Brady asked.

'No,' Thomas replied. He kicked out at the wall. 'This is ridiculous,' he said, spitting the words out. 'How are we ever going to get out of here? We've no idea whether we're any closer to the exit or not. How did you manage it last time, you pair?' he asked Brady and Ella. 'How in the heck did you get out of this maze?'

'We've already told you,' Ella said. 'We don't know. We just kept moving and eventually found the exit.'

'Speaking of keeping moving,' Brady said. 'I don't think it's a good idea to linger in one spot for too long.'

He led the way, moving off at pace.

As they continued exploring the maze, Finlay said to Thomas: 'So ... does this mean that I can use your XBOX now without you having a meltdown? And does it mean that I can play with your toys as well, without you whinging or getting me in a headlock?'

Thomas opened his mouth to reply. He was about to tell Finlay to get lost, but then he reconsidered. What if the wizard could hear what they were saying?

Thomas had promised to be a good boy and, essentially, be kind to his brother. That promise, however, had been based on the wizard not zapping him with his wand. Promises or not, the wizard had been about to cast a spell anyway.

'Well?' Finlay said. 'If we ever get out of this place, can I use your XBOX without you throwing a tizzy, or not?'

'I can't believe you're worried about something like that at a time like this,' Thomas said. 'Yes, you can use it. Anything to shut you up.'

'I'll hold you to that,' Finlay said, taking the lead position. This surprised Thomas, because Finlay had admitted that he wasn't keen on the dark. And yet there he was, surging ahead through the passages. Since Brady wasn't having any luck finding a way out, nobody voiced an objection.

Fifteen minutes passed before anything else happened. Finlay was still at the front. He was humming to himself: no doubt trying to take his mind off things, Thomas figured. Ella was bringing up the rear, and it was she who heard the noises.

'Shhh!' she said, raising a finger and bringing everyone to a stop.

They all listened, but they couldn't hear anything.

'What is it?' Thomas asked her. 'What did you hear?'

'*Shhhh!*' she said again. This time more forcefully.

Again, they all listened – but this time they heard

it:

Footsteps!

On the far wall, across from the passage they'd just walked down, a shadow began to form.

'It's him!' Thomas said. 'It's the wizard!'

A hand appeared, holding a wand ...

The others didn't need prompting to flee. Finlay took off like a hundred metre sprinter, his little legs moving at blurring speed. Thomas had never seen him go so fast. Brady grabbed Ella's hand and Thomas shepherded them along. Then he followed behind them, close on their heels. Just before Thomas disappeared around the corner, he glanced over his shoulder and caught a glimpse of those glowing eyes.

Inevitably, after exploring numerous passages, they hit a dead end. They backtracked as fast as they could, hoping desperately that they wouldn't get boxed-in by the wizard. As luck would have it, they didn't. They continued to explore, still moving with life-dependent urgency – until, finally, they came to a door, which had a riddle on it.

'This is it!' Brady said, breathing hard because he was so out of breath. 'This *must* be the way out!'

'Another riddle,' Ella said, rolling her eyes.

'If solving it gets us out of here,' Thomas said, 'then that can only be a good thing.'

Finlay read it out loud: 'I'm big and green and scaly. My teeth are sharp as knives. My tail is long and can whip you fast. My wings are vast, so I can take great flight. The fire I breathe can light up the night. What am I?'

'There's only one thing I can think of that breathes fire,' Brady said ominously, 'and that's a dragon.'

'It does fit with the rest of the riddle,' Finlay said. 'They're big and green and have sharp teeth. Their tales are long and their wings are vast. But I still hope you're wrong. Please tell me we aren't going to have to battle a *dragon!* I mean, of all things ... a *DRAGON!*'

The door clicked open, which was answer enough.

'O-kay,' Ella said. 'So who's going first?'

'After you,' Thomas said, gesturing the others to go before him.

'Oh, no,' Brady said, returning the gesture, 'after you.'

Ella held up a finger and shushed everyone. 'I think I hear something.'

Everyone listened, wanting to know what she had thought she'd just heard. Thomas had a good idea what it was and a bad sense of déjà vu seized him. And then they all heard it:

Footsteps!

A shadow began to form on the wall at the end of the passage.

'It's the w-w-wizard!' Ella cried, stuttering.

Flinging the door open, Thomas grabbed her by the arm and bundled her through. Brady and Finlay did not need prompting to follow her. They tried to get through the doorway at the same time and got stuck. Thomas gave them a shove and they both went sprawling to their hands and knees. Just before Thomas disappeared through the door and shut it behind him, he couldn't resist looking down the passage. All he could make out in the darkness was the wizard's balefully glowing eyes bearing down on him ...

Thomas slammed the door and put his back against it, pushing with every bit of strength he could muster. Then the others gathered around him, pushing against it as well.

Beginning

End

CHAPTER FIVE

(Fire and Heroics)

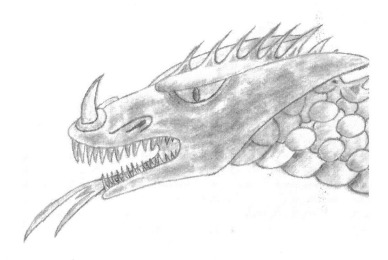

'Is that it?' Brady said. 'Did we win the second task?'

Since Thomas was the only one facing away from the door, he was the only one who could see what was in the room they'd just entered. He stared dead ahead as if he'd been hypnotized.

'I do believe we've just evened the score,' Finlay said, continuing to push as hard as he could against the door. 'D'you think we're okay to move away from here now, Thomas? The wizard shouldn't be after us if we've won ... should he?'

'I'm starting to develop a severe dislike for the word "if",' Ella said.

Thomas continued to stare ahead, still looking hypnotized. Then he muttered, 'Please be quiet – we don't want to wake it up.'

Following his gaze, the others craned their necks to look around, so they could see what Thomas was seeing.

'Oh ... my ... *god*,' Brady whispered, backing away as much as he could. 'Please tell me that I'm seeing things and that that isn't what I think it is.'

'If you're seeing things, then so am I,' Finlay said, his voice full of jitters.

Ella's mouth had dropped open. She looked like she was struggling for words, but then she suddenly found her voice: 'Erm, I'm thinking that going back into the maze isn't such a bad idea right now.'

'That's not an option,' Thomas said, making his way past the others.

'What are you doing?' Brady said, continuing to hold the door. 'Get back over here – the wizard might try to get through.'

'If he wants to get through, do you think we'd be able to stop him?' Thomas said.

'That's a fair point,' Brady admitted, but he still continued to hold the door, as did the others.

Thomas looked over his shoulder at them. 'Forget about that – forget about the wizard.' He nodded forwards. 'We need to concentrate on him ... and how we're going to get past *him*.'

He surveyed the cavernous space before him and everything that was in it. An assortment of spaced out padded upright tumble boards filled most of the room. Some of the boards had cannon-like ball shooters mounted on top of them, which looked capable of dealing stinging blows. Beyond this, at the back of the room, set high up on a raised floor, was a huge dragon. At the moment it was sleeping, snoring loudly with its chin resting on its clawed paws. The dragon was exactly as the riddle had described: green and scaly. Its vast wings were tucked tight against the girth of its body. Around its neck was a plastic chain, which was secured to the wall behind it. A door to the left of the beast caught Thomas's eye. *That's it*, he thought – *that's the way out*.

'And there's an X,' he said, pointing at one of the boards. *Like we needed conformation that this is the last main challenge*, he thought.

By now, the others had firmly realised that there was no point in trying to keep the wizard from entering via the door that led to the maze. Brady, Finlay and Ella had joined Thomas at his side, taking in the task that was ahead of them.

'If that thing wakes up, we're goners,' Finlay said. 'As if that plastic chain is going to stop it from getting at us. One good lunge and it'll break, I bet.'

'I wouldn't be so sure,' Thomas said, keeping his voice low. 'The armour I wore was made from plastic and that was as hard as a tortoise shell. Things are different in here, remember. Although how long it'll hold it back is anyone's guess.' He nodded towards the door. 'We need to get through there, because I'm pretty sure it's the way out.'

'This should be easy,' Brady said, 'if the overgrown lizard doesn't wake up.'

'There's that word again,' Ella said. '*If.*'

Thomas pinched his index finger and thumb together, then ran them across his lips, mimicking a zipping gesture. '*Please* keep it quiet. If that thing *does* wake up, things could get very hot in here.'

'It's chained up,' Finlay said, 'so it won't be able to get to us until we're near the platform.'

'Dragons breathe fire,' Brady pointed out, 'so it *can* get us.'

'But if it breathes fire,' Ella said, 'won't it burn the place down?'

'I would have thought so,' Finlay concurred.

Thomas pulled the note from his pocket and read the last part: 'Lose on the other hand and things could get heated. You'll disappear in the blink of an eye as if you've been deleted.'

'So if we lose we'll be heated by the dragon's fire

and deleted,' Finlay said.

'It doesn't say we'll be deleted,' Ella said, correcting him. 'It says we'll disappear *as if* we've been deleted.'

'Oh well that sounds much more promising,' Finlay said sarcastically. He motioned towards one of the shooters. 'As if that's going to do *anything* to a dragon. It'll be like firing Nerf bullets at an elephant. And what do those things fire anyway? If it's the normal soft balls you get in a play centre, then why even bother?'

Thomas glared at him. 'Keep the noise *down*,' he said, his voice a low, harsh sting. 'Do you really want that thing to wake up?' He took a deep breath and composed himself. 'Okay, we need to think about how we're going to do this ...'

'Splitting into two groups would be a good idea,' Brady said. 'That way, if the worst comes to the worst, one group can distract it while the other makes progress.'

'Sounds good to me,' Thomas said.

Pocketing the note, he edged forwards, closer to the padded boards. From this vantage point, he could now see what was behind one of them: a bag full of nice surprises. 'Dreadbolts,' Thomas said, advancing towards the bag. He pulled out one of the crossbows and held it up. 'Not sure how effective these will be, but I'd rather have them than not. There's lots of Nerf arrows in here as well.'

'If firing those at the beast doesn't work,' Ella said,

'we could always try tickling it.'

'I don't think they'd be here if they weren't going to do anything,' Brady said, sneering at her. 'And you don't have to use one if you don't want to. You can just hide behind the boards while we do all the brave stuff, if you like?'

'There's no need to be like that,' Ella hissed.

Thomas noticed that her hands were shaking. She was scared; he could see that. But then they were all scared, Thomas included. As terrified as he was, though, he was equally determined. He and the others had gotten through the first two major challenges, plus the minor ones, without sustaining any serious injuries. He was damn sure they could get through this one if they worked together as a team.

'There must be ammunition for the shooters as well,' Finlay said, moving towards the nearest board that had a cannon on top. 'Not good news, I'm afraid. They *do* shoot soft balls. There's a box full of them down here. There's a box full of them at every cannon, I think.'

'I don't think they'd be here if they weren't going do anything,' Ella said, mimicking what Brady had said earlier.

Thomas was about to tell her to keep her voice down again, but then a siren rang out from somewhere in the room, cutting him off. For the few seconds that it sounded, Thomas and the others exchanged worried looks. When it died away, they turned their attention towards the dragon, which was now opening its serpentine eyes.

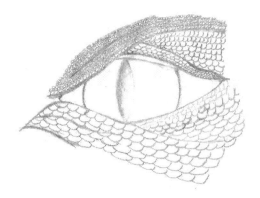

'Why did I know something like that was going to happen,' Brady said.

From somewhere inside the room a motorized noise kicked in and the whooshing sound of air flowing could be heard all around them.

Then the dragon raised its head and got slowly to its feet, looking around. It noticed the children and let out a ferocious roar, displaying all its razor-sharp teeth.

'Oh poop,' Finlay said, backing away and looking terrified. '*Oh poop-di-poop!*'

'Now might be a good time to take cover,' Thomas advised.

He ducked down behind nearest board and the others followed suit. Brady and Ella crouched next to him and Finlay put his back against the one with the cannon on top.

'Perhaps if we stay here for long enough he might forget about us,' Brady said.

'He'll remember soon enough when you pop your head back up,' Thomas said.

Reaching into the bag, Ella pulled out one of the Dreadbolts and a handful of arrows. 'May as well be ready,' she said.

Thomas took it from her and placed an arrow into the chamber. Arrows could be stored horizontally on the top of the crossbow, so he clipped five in place for easy loading.

'Have you ever fired one of these?' Thomas asked Ella and Brady.

'We've got plenty of Nerf guns at home,' Brady replied, 'but, no, we've never fired a Dreadbolt.'

'It's easy,' Thomas said. He pulled the lever down on the bottom of the crossbow and it snapped back into its original position, tight against the underside. 'That's it – it's that simple. Locked and loaded. Idiot-proof.'

Brady and Ella readied themselves with crossbows, so that they were locked and loaded.

'We're quite far away,' Thomas said, 'so make sure you aim above the target to compensate for the distance.'

Brady and Ella nodded in unison.

Thomas was about to turn his attention to his brother, but the dragon let out a ferocious roar, which made Thomas's blood run cold. He could hear the dragon pulling at its chain as it padded across the platform, desperate to get at its prey.

'It's going to let go with the heat as soon as it sees us,' Thomas said.

'I think the whooshing sound we heard was the air going to the cannons,' Brady said. 'Which means we should be able to fire those now.'

Thomas was about to convey this information to Finlay, but Finlay already had some balls in his hands and looked ready to load them.

'You three move forwards and I'll cover you,' he said.

Thomas didn't like the idea of his brother being exposed to danger – especially the sort of danger that might get him flame-grilled. But there was no way around this – no safe way for any of them to advance. They *all* needed to move forwards and they *all* needed to get through the door.

'Okay,' Thomas said to Finlay, 'but be careful.'

Finlay gave him a nod. 'And you be careful, too. All of you.'

'We'll advance to the next board, no further,' Thomas said to Brady and Ella.

They nodded to show they understood.

Thomas could see that Ella's hands were still shaking. This time her brother noticed as well.

'It's all right,' Brady said, putting a hand on her shoulder. 'Just stick with us and we'll be okay.'

'Oh don't you worry about me,' she replied, raising her chin in the air defiantly. 'Yes I'm scared, but we're going to show that dragon what for, aren't we?'

'You betcha,' Brady said, giving her a wink.

'Okay,' Thomas said. 'On my count: 3 ... 2 ... 1 ... *let's go!*'

As he broke cover, Finlay rose and began loading balls into the cannon. They shot out at an amazing speed, trailing sparkling blue dust behind them as they went. When the first one hit home, pinging off the side of the dragon's head, it exploded in a cloud of blue dust. Other shots went wide, exploding against the wall at the far end. This gave the dragon the chance to recover from the initial blast, which had stunned it slightly. Opening its cavernous mouth, it showcased its teeth, which reminded Thomas of stalagmites and stalactites: long, pointy and sharp. Fortunately, by this time, Thomas and the others had reached the next board and taken cover.

As a blast of fire erupted above their heads, Thomas yelled, '*GET DOWN!*'

He couldn't see Finlay from his position, but there'd been no yelp of pain to suggest he'd been injured, or fatally hurt.

'I'm all right!' Finlay called out.

Thomas could not remember ever feeling so relieved in his life. His brother could be annoying sometimes and Thomas could think of many occasions when he could quite happily have throttled him. But the thought of anything truly bad happening to Finlay made Thomas feel sick with worry. And now it was Finlay's turn to run the gauntlet while the others provided cover.

'That's weird,' Brady said. 'I didn't feel any heat. With a blast of fire like that, we should have felt like we were being toasted.'

'If there's no heat then maybe it won't burn us if we get hit with a blast,' Ella speculated.

'I'm not sure I want to put that theory to the test,' Thomas said. 'It's blowing fire for a reason.'

'To make us disappear as though we've been deleted?' Brady said.

'That could well be the case,' Thomas replied.

'Disappear?' Ella said, alarmed. 'Where to?'

Good question, Thomas thought. *Is it going to teleport us somewhere, or are we just going to disappear, full stop – as if we've been deleted.* He turned his attention to Finlay. 'Okay, it's your turn. Just let us know when you're ready and we'll open fire.'

Brady and Ella nodded to signify they were all set.

'I wonder if these crossbow arrows will be charged with the blue stuff,' Brady said, 'like the cannon balls.'

'We're about to find out,' Thomas said.

'On the count of three again,' Finlay said. '3 ... 2 ... 1 ... *go!*'

All standing at the same time, Thomas, Brady and Ella took aim and leased off their arrows. Thomas and Brady's went high and wide, troubling nothing but the wall. Ella's, however, was on target. It struck the dragon in the chest, exploding in a cloud of blue dust, just like the foam cannon ball (except with less impact). It didn't harm the dragon very much, as far as Thomas could tell. But it did distract it long enough for Finlay to get to safety, behind the next board. The downside to this, of course, was that the dragon turned its attention fully towards the others. As it opened its mouth to unleash another blast of heatless fire, they ducked down out of harm's way.

Flames erupted over their heads.

Thank God the Nerf arrows hadn't been charged with that blue stuff when me and Finlay crossed that beam, Thomas thought. He remembered how Mr Tinkler had explained what adrenaline was. *I bet I've got plenty of that flowing through my body at the moment. I can feel it!*

Brady said. 'How many times are we going to have to do this before we reach that door?'

'I counted six boards between us and that platform before we began,' Thomas responded. 'Crikey, can you hear him tugging at that chain. I swear it's going to snap in a minute, and then the fun *really* will begin.'

'Wizard or not, I'll be heading back into the maze if *that* happens,' Ella said.

Brady said, 'It must be made of really strong plastic is all I can say. To hold a beast of that size, it must be.'

'I don't like how Finlay is on his own,' Thomas

said, shaking his head in frustration. 'I should never have let that happen. Perhaps I should go to him. What do you think?'

'He's doing fine on his own,' Brady said. 'We're taking enough risks here already, without adding in any unnecessary extra ones.'

'He's only broken cover once,' Thomas said. 'He's going to have to do it another five times – on his own.'

'If you want to go to him, then fine,' Brady said. 'We'll cover you. But I still think it's an unnecessary risk.'

Thomas looked towards his brother, asking a question with his expression. Finlay shook his head slowly and mouthed the words: 'No, don't – I'm fine.'

'Perhaps we should try to get further this time,' Brady said. 'Go two boards instead of one.'

Ella could see the folly in this suggestion. 'We just nearly got blasted moving to one,' she said. 'You were talking about unnecessary risks just now, remember?'

'She's right,' Thomas agreed. 'Moving more than one at a time would be too dangerous.'

'How's your brother going to cover us now?' Brady said, nodding in Finlay's direction. 'He's not at a board that has a cannon and he hasn't got a crossbow.'

Finlay was looking in their direction, no doubt wondering what they were talking about.

Thomas held his Dreadbolt up and then tossed it in Finlay's direction. He caught it with ease.

'Now you don't have one,' Brady said.

'You and Ella need to make sure you hit the target, then, don't you?' Thomas said.

'Your shot was the one that went the widest,' Ella pointed out.

'Whatever,' Thomas said, trying to concentrate on what needed to be done. 'The next board we're going to has a cannon on top.'

The dragon let out an eardrum-shattering roar. It pulled at its chain again.

Then Finlay loaded an arrow into the chamber of his crossbow and signalled he was ready.

Thomas couldn't help but admire his brother. He was clearly petrified, but he was battling on anyway. Prior to this adventure, Thomas would never have believed that Finlay could be so brave. Thomas felt proud of him again.

'On the count of three again,' Thomas said to the others. '3 ... 2 ... 1 ... *go!*'

Brady and Ella went first, leasing off shots as they broke cover. Brady's missed the target and so did Ella's. Fortunately, Finlay's hit the mark, disappearing straight down the dragon's throat as it opened its mouth to breathe another bout of fire. Closing its mouth with a snap, the dragon's eyes widened as it took a few stumbling steps forwards, clearly struggling.

Reaching the next board, Thomas brought Brady and Ella to a halt, but none of them ducked for cover this time. They were too busy watching the dragon, which was padding back and forth on the platform, choking up some vile, yellow liquid.

'What are we waiting for?' Brady said. 'This is our chance!'

He and Ella began moving forwards at pace. Thomas turned to tell Finlay to do the same, but Finlay was already bounding towards him.

'That was a heck of a shot,' Thomas said to his brother as they took off after the others. 'You were aiming for its mouth, right?'

'Of course I was,' Finlay replied, but the look on his face suggested otherwise.

The four of them made it all the way to one of the boards near the front of the room before the dragon finally got itself under control. Rearing up on its hind legs, it spread its wings to their full extent and fixed the kids with a baleful stare. Thomas was amazed by the vastness of its wingspan, which must have been forty feet from the tip of one to the other.

Once again, the children took cover.

'Damn,' Brady said, 'we nearly made it all the way.'

'Get another one in its mouth and we will,' Ella said. 'Especially one of those cannon balls.'

'Erm,' Finlay said, looking solemn, 'I don't want to be the bringer of bad news, but did anyone else notice that there was golden writing on that door?'

'Oh you're kidding, right?' Thomas said. 'Tell me you're kidding.'

'As if I would at a time like *this*,' Finlay responded.

'Another riddle,' Brady said, shaking his head. 'How are we s'pposed to solve a riddle *and* battle a dragon at the same time?'

'With great difficulty,' Ella said.

'So what is the plan?' Brady said.

Thomas realised that everyone was looking at him, which made him feel uncomfortable. *They want me to come up with a solution*, he thought. *Like I'm their leader or something.* 'I think the best suggestion has already been made. Ella is spot on. We nearly made it all the way because an arrow went down the beast's throat. Imagine what a cannon ball will do.'

'Would it kill it, d'you think?' Finlay asked. 'I know it's trying to burn us alive – or make us disappear, or whatever – but I don't want to kill it.'

'I think it'll take a bit more than that,' Ella stated.

Careful to keep low, Thomas looked around, locating the nearest board with a cannon on top. He nodded towards it. 'One of us needs to run for that. Who's got the best aim?'

'Your brother found the target once,' Brady said to him. 'Maybe he can do it again.'

'It was a lucky shot,' Finlay admitted. 'I was aiming for its chest.'

'My shot wasn't lucky,' Ella said. 'I aimed for the dragon's chest and hit it.'

Brady did not look comfortable with the idea of his sister running the gauntlet without him. 'I could go

120

with you,' he suggested.

'I didn't say I was going to do it,' Ella said, backtracking on the idea. 'I was just ... pointing out that if I can do it, then you guys can too.'

'Of course you were,' Brady said, rolling his eyes.

Ella snapped: 'Don't roll your eyes at me, you numnit! You know I hate it when you do that.'

'Don't call me a numnit!' Brady snapped back at her. 'I've warned you about *that* before.'

'Now is not the time for family squabbles,' Thomas said.

The dragon roared as if in agreement.

'So who's doing this, then?' Finlay enquired. 'It's a shame we can't draw straws.'

'I'll do it,' Thomas said. 'Anything to stop you pair from bickering.'

'But you haven't hit the target once yet,' Ella said.

Thomas said, 'I'm about due, then, aren't I?'

'I hope so,' Ella muttered, looking uncertain.

'When I'm in position, you lot keep peppering it with shots,' Thomas said. 'Make it roar as much as you can and make sure you take cover after each attack. We're very close to the creature now, so you won't have as much time to react should it blast fire at you.'

He risked a quick peek over the board, then reported what he'd seen back to the others. 'It's crouched low. Looks ready to pounce.'

'Which it will do,' Finlay said, 'if that chain doesn't

hold.'

'Okay ...' Thomas said, summoning up the courage for the dash. He took a long, deep breath and exhaled. 'Okay ... o-*kay*.'

'When you've got to do something that scares you,' Brady said, 'I always find it's best not to hesitate. That's when doubts creep in. Just have at it, I say.'

Easier said than done when there's a dragon involved, Thomas thought. But he could see Brady's point.

'Okay ...' Thomas said, psyching himself up. 'Once again, on my count: 3 ... 2 ... 1 ... *go!*'

He bolted away like a grey hound out of its trap. Snatching a glance sideways, he saw the dragon rearing up, opening its mouth, ready to release a blast of flames. Before it could do so, however, three Nerf arrows exploded on its body, driving it backwards.

Reaching the board with the cannon, Thomas slid in behind it and smiled to himself. He looked towards the others, expecting to see that all three of them had taken cover. But only Brady and Finlay were crouched low. Ella was still standing up, trying to load another arrow into her Dreadbolt.

'What are you doing?' Brady said. 'Get down!'

'It's stunned,' Ella said. She continued trying to load the arrow, but her hands were shaking so much that she just couldn't manage it.

'Thomas has made it,' Finlay said to her, 'so get *down!*'

The beast had been rocked quite badly by the triple

shot, but it was now beginning to recover.

Ella had finally managed to load the arrow into her Dreadbolt. She went to take aim, then realised that the dragon was staring her dead in the eyes.

Thomas was watching this spectacle unfold with disbelief and a growing sense of horror. *'Get DOWN!'* he yelled.

A ferocious blast of fire erupted from the dragon's mouth. For a split second, Thomas was sure that Ella was about to be engulfed. But then Brady and Finlay reached up at the same time and yanked her to the floor, out of harm's way.

'Well that wasn't stupid at all,' Finlay said, glaring at her.

'You could have died!' Brady said, wading in as well.

Ella looked like she didn't know whether to cry or erupt in a fit of anger. She opted for the latter. 'It was *hurt*,' she seethed. 'I was just trying to take advantage of that. And if this *blumin'* crossbow hadn't have jammed, I would have.' She slammed the Dreadbolt to the floor and a piece snapped off the side.

'Very clever!' Brady said, chiding her. 'Like we don't need that!'

'I can't believe she did that,' Finlay said.

Thomas had heard enough. 'Will you pipe down, you three!' he said. 'Forget about what just happened and concentrate on what we have to do next!'

This silenced them. No more words were

exchanged: just dirty looks.

And then Brady veered things back in the right direction. 'Me and Finlay will distract the dragon while you fire your balls,' he said to Thomas. 'Make 'em count.' He turned his attention to his sister. 'You'll just have to keep low and be ready to move when we give the shout.'

She did not look happy about this. But she didn't voice any protest.

'I really hope this is the last time I have to do this count down,' Thomas said. He inhaled, holding his breath, then he exhaled, steadying himself. '3 ... 2 ... 1 ... *go!*'

Thomas watched as the other two rose and then, a split second later, he rose, too. The first thing to go wrong was that neither Brady nor Finlay hit their target. Despite their close proximity to the dragon, both of their shots missed narrowly (mainly due to the fact that the dragon was moving around so much). The second thing to go wrong was that Thomas missed the target as well. Not only did he not get the cannon ball down the dragon's throat, he didn't even trouble it with a strike to the body or head. The ball sailed high and wide by a good few feet. The third and final thing to go wrong was ... Ella.

She had peeked around the side of the board and seen what'd happened. Clearly not impressed by the others and their efforts to shoot the beast, she decided that she could do better. Rising up like a Jack out of a

124

box, she attempted to snatch Finlay's Dreadbolt from him. But he was having not of it.

'What are you doing?' he said, trying to push her away.

'I can do better,' she replied, continuing with her efforts to take the crossbow from him. 'I *won't* miss.'

Thomas could see that a disaster was about to take place, so he yelled, '*TAKE COVER – GET DOWN!*'

Brady was trying to wrestle them apart. 'Are you pair for real?' he said, struggling to get in-between them. 'Now *really* is not the time for something like this!'

Pulling its chain as taught as it could be, the dragon set itself and began opening its mouth to unleash a blast.

Thomas considered loading another ball into the cannon, but he knew he couldn't risk missing with the shot.

He realised there was only one thing left to do. He darted across the room, yelling '*GET DOWWWWN!*' as he went. Brady had given up on his brief attempt at trying to separate Finlay and Ella. He was now trying to drag both of them down, but not having much luck. This all happened in less than a few seconds, but to Thomas it felt like much longer. Getting to within a couple of feet of the others, he saw flames erupt from the dragon's mouth. Throwing himself through the air, Thomas landed on Brady's back, driving him forwards and down. The two of them then collided

125

with Finlay and Ella, knocking them to floor, behind the safety of the board.

Or, at least, that's what Thomas thought at first. As the flaming blast exploded around them, enveloping their area, Thomas noticed that Ella's legs, from the knees downwards, were protruding beyond the far end of the board. Before he could even think about doing anything about this, however, the flames engulfed her ankles. Cringing and looking away, Thomas braced himself for the inevitable scream that was about to erupt from Ella's throat. But she did not scream, or cry out in pain, or even whimper. Thomas looked back at her just as the flames were dying away and he was amazed to see that the bottom half of her legs had *disappeared*. He shook his head, sure that what he was seeing was some form of hallucination. He thought: *what the ... heck!* Then the last sentence on the note echoed in his mind: ... disappear ... disappear ... as if you've been deleted ...

Thomas grabbed Ella and yanked her towards him.

'*Are you totally nuts!*' Brady screamed at her. And then he noticed what'd happened to her legs as well.

'Erm ...' Finlay said, aghast, pointing. 'I think you're missing something, Ella.'

A look of horror spread across her face as she noticed what the others had noticed.

'My ... legs,' she said, her voice barely a whisper. Her mouth dropped open in shock. She let rip with a scream. '*WHERE ARE MY LEGS!*'

Thomas was about to tell Ella to calm down (for all the good *that* would have done) when he observed that her legs were beginning to materialise again.

'They're coming back, look,' he said, pointing. 'They're coming back!'

Ella began flapping her hands, like a bird that was desperately trying to fly and couldn't. She looked torn between being relieved and being horrified.

'Just stay calm,' Brady said, taking one of her hands and squeezing it tightly. 'They're coming back, so just keep your cool and everything will be okay.'

'She should be burned – her legs should be *burned* – so why aren't they?' Finlay said. 'Why have they disappeared instead?' And then he got it. 'That explains why there's no heat. The fire isn't meant to burn us. We were right about it being meant to make us disappear, though ...'

'... as if we've been deleted,' Thomas said.

'Oh man, that's just creepy,' Finlay said, shuddering visibly.

Ella's legs were nearly back to normal. They'd almost fully materialised again. As she sat looking at them, tears were rolling down her cheeks and her shoulders were hitching up and down uncontrollably.

'What's going on?' she said, hardly able to breathe. 'What ... What just happened to me?' She was still too hysterical to have processed the conclusion that Thomas and Finlay had come to.

Thomas said to her: 'The fire isn't meant to burn

us; it's meant to make us disappear.'

'If that's the case,' Brady said, 'then why are the bottom of my sister's legs reappearing?'

They'd fully re-materialised now. Ella touched them tentatively at first, then ran her fingers up and down them, from her knees to her ankles.

'They're back!' she said, smiling through the tears. '*They're back!*'

'Yes,' Thomas said. 'But why?'

'What do you mean, why?' Brady said. 'Who cares *why!*'

A blast of fire erupted above their heads, making them all duck. The dragon once again roared, tugging at its chain and padding around on the platform.

'Thomas has a point,' Finlay said. 'He's right to ask why. What's the point of the creature making us disappear if all that's going to happen is that we reappear? Unless ... unless ...' He clicked his fingers together, pondering this quandary.

But it was Brady who came up with the answer. 'Unless ... the dragon needs to make us disappear entirely. It may need to engulf our bodies entirely with fire for that to happen.'

This conclusion was greeted with sombre looks.

'And what happens then?' Ella said, biting down on her bottom lip whilst rubbing her red, glistening eyes. 'What happens after we disappear?'

Good question, Thomas thought. 'Let's just make sure that doesn't happen,' he said.

'No more silliness from you would help,' Brady said to his sister, chastising her. 'You nearly got *vaporised* because of what you did. What were you thinking? Please promise me you won't do something like that again.'

'If you lot hadn't been useless with your shooting, then I wouldn't have had to try and get involved,' Ella replied sulkily.

Thomas held up a hand in a calming gesture. 'Let's forget about that now,' he said. 'Let's concentrate on how we're getting to that door without anyone getting vaporised – as Brady put it – or transported to another dimension, or another world, or something ...'

'D'you think that's what'll happen to us?' Finlay said. 'If we get caught in the fire – *fully* caught – we'll end up in another dimension?'

Prior to today, Thomas would have dismissed this idea as ludicrous. But after everything that'd happened in the last hour or so, nothing would surprise him. The thought of this was slightly more appealing than just vanishing outright. Even if they did end up in another dimension, at least they would still be alive.

Thomas peeked around the side of the board, so he could gauge the distance between themselves and the door. Unfortunately, the sight of him sent the dragon into a frenzied fit. Flapping its wings, it lunged forwards with such force that the chain around its neck came away from the wall with a *snap!*

'Oh no!' Thomas said, ducking back behind the board. 'Oh no no *no NO!*'

'Please tell me that snapping sound wasn't what I think it was?' Brady said.

'It was,' Thomas replied. 'We need to run back to the maze. Everyone follow me. Don't look back – just *run*. Fast as you can!'

'But what about the wizard?' Ella said.

No time to answer that question. Thomas hoisted the others up and got them moving. Finlay snatched up a Dreadbolt as he led the way.

'Run run *RUN!*' Thomas said, following after them.

They didn't get very far. After half a dozen steps, a mighty roar echoed throughout the room. And that was the last thing they heard from the dragon. Fire erupted all around them: engulfing Thomas first and then the others. Ella screamed, even though there was no pain. The others screamed, too: more in surprise than anything else.

As Thomas looked down at himself and saw his body disappearing, thoughts raced through his head. He wondered what would happen next. *Is this really it? Am I about to die? Or am I being whisked off to some other place, some other world, some other when and where?* A third, hopeful option popped into his head: *Maybe we're being teleported back to the play centre.* But he couldn't see this being the case. They'd only won one of the three main tasks that'd been set for them. Surely there would be no reward for failure, no reward for losing. They hadn't got close enough to the door to read what the riddle had said, but Thomas would have bet his XBOX that he could have figured out what the answer would have been ...

Home.

Thomas watched as the others in front of him began to disappear as well. His attention was focused mostly on his brother, whom he felt like he had failed. *I'm sorry, Finlay*, he thought. *Sorry I led you into this.* The fire raged around all of them. Arms and legs and bodies and heads disappeared – until nothing but a flaming inferno filled Thomas's vision.

And then, through it all, as the flames began to subside (along with Ella's screams) Thomas saw that the others were reappearing. He heard Finlay's voice: 'I can see something ahead,' he said, sounding awestruck. 'Oh wow ... *wow*, look at that!'

Ella said, *'Wowww!'*

Brady said something, but Thomas only caught one word: awesome.

And then Thomas surged ahead, eager to see what the others were seeing ...

Author note:

Quite often, I get asked where I get the ideas for my stories. It'll probably come as no surprise to you that the idea for this one came from a visit to a soft play centre. My three year old loves going, but my eight year old always protests, saying that it's boring (and that he'd rather muck about on his XBOX). One day, whilst playing a game of hide and seek with them at a play centre we'd never been to before, I noticed a small door at the rear of the room, tucked away in the corner. This set my imagination going. I wondered what could be behind that door, and things just went from there. This book is just the beginning of what will be a very big adventure. I hope you enjoyed reading it, because I sure did have a lot of fun writing it.

PJJ

Please visit https://www.facebook.com/pjjovanovic for updates on further books in this series.

Also from Paul Johnson-Jovanovic:

If you like Harry Potter, you'll love this.

A spellbinding wizard school adventure novel ...

Alfie Trotter is no ordinary boy. He can do things other children can't. He can turn the telly over just by thinking it. He can make lights flicker on and off when he gets angry. He can make objects disappear, never to be seen again. He knows why he's able to do these things, because his parents have told him that he's a wizard. What Alfie doesn't know, however, is that there's a magic school for children just like him.

But all that is about to change as Alfie meets a boy named Charles, who recognizes him for what he is. Charles tells him about the Pendred Academy of Magic and before long Alfie finds himself enrolling for his first lesson. Whilst there, Alfie learns of a plot by an evil wizard to steal a powerful wand, which is being stored in a safe at the academy. He also finds out that the academy grounds serve as a portal: a gateway to another world. And that's when the real adventure begins …

FEELS LIKE MAGIC is part one of a projected five book series.

Read what Amazon reviewers are saying:

"Great. I read it through in one sitting. Looking forward to the next one. Very similar to Harry Potter."

"I liked the characters and it was fun to read. I was sad when it ended, I want the rest of the story."

"Feels Like Magic is the first book of a great adventure, the characters in the book are likeable and interesting. They are plunged into new and exciting worlds when they discover magic. There is a generosity of spirit and kindness extended between friends in the book and we are caught up in the tension created in some of the situations they find themselves in. We look forward to the next book."

"Awesome book. Can't wait to read more from this author."

Get your copy of **FEELS LIKE MAGIC** and let the magical adventure begin. You won't be disappointed …